Down to You

Lauren Lieberman

Dedication

For my mom, who always believed that I would write a book one day.

CHAPTER 1

WINTER 2016

As I sit here 39,000 feet in the air nursing a mimosa on the plane to Cozumel, I can't help but laugh at the turn my life has taken. Or else I would cry—and I am not a cute crier by any means. I'm also not a bitter person by nature, but when you're attending your brother's wedding in a tropical paradise as the only single guest, it's inevitable that some of your joy for the happy couple will be a teensy bit tainted. I did anticipate that this situation would sting a bit, but when we started planning this blessed event only weeks ago, I thought that maybe, just *maybe* I would miraculously have a date. Or even a booty call. Or at least someone to drunk-dial on the night of! But, lo and behold, I am indeed attending alone, knowing he will be there. Lucas, my childhood crush, my ex (if you can even call him that), the love of my life.

The flight attendant sees my grimace and asks if there's anything she can do for me.

I give her a pained smile. "What do you have to get

me through a three-day wedding in Mexico where the man who obliterated my heart is one of two groomsmen?"

Without a word, she hands me another mimosa.

I nod in gratitude, finish the first one in a single gulp, and pass her back the empty glass. I sink back in my seat and sigh loudly—which, judging by the expression on the older gentleman next to me, is something I've been doing repeatedly for the past hour.

I try to clear my head, but sure enough, thoughts of Lucas creep back in. Our romance had an unconventional start: he's one of my older brother's best friends, and I'm the off-limits younger sister. But somehow, to my delight, it did happen—albeit briefly—before it spectacularly blew up in my face. Twice. And it will probably be the epic love story of my lifetime. *And also my downfall*, I think as I start in on my second drink.

I catch the flight attendant's eye and tell her to keep the mimosas coming.

I step off the plane and am immediately slapped with a wall of humidity that makes it impossible to suck in a breath. I pull my sunglasses down over my eyes and raise my hand to my face to shield myself from the blazing Mexican sun threatening to burn my retinas. Jesus, it's hot.

There's no bridge leading the disembarking passengers from the plane into the airport; everyone descends a set of metal stairs on wheels to reach the tarmac. I close my eyes and say a quick prayer that I don't tumble to my death before I follow suit, making my way down the flimsy steps. Sweat has already begun to bead at my brow and between my shoulder blades. Thank God I dressed in layers, I think as I pull off my hoodie.

Men hand out Coronas in front of the airport doors. I grab one, wishing it was a margarita, but grateful for the cold bottle as I touch it to my forehead before taking a giant gulp. I'm hoping to awaken the mimosa buzz I started on the first half of the flight.

I follow the rest of the passengers into the terminal, where a huge line zigzags the length of the room, waiting to pass through customs. *Great.* I sigh, fanning myself with my passport. It must be a hundred degrees in here. The line moves at a snail's pace, and now I feel the sweat trickling between my boobs. Damn, I wish I'd grabbed two beers from that guy. I drain the last sip and toss the bottle into a nearby trash can. My brother Jake and his bride-to-be, Ashley, who also happens to be my best friend since kindergarten, have assured me that my room at the hotel will have a fully stocked minibar, and they'd better be right if I'm going to get through the next few days. The two of them, along with both sets of our parents, came down yesterday on a sold-out flight, hence my solo trip today. Which was fine with me; it gave me an extra day to prepare myself and gather my nerves to see "he who must not be named." Another day to practice my happy face as the supportive maid of honor for my best friend and brother.

This whirlwind wedding came together in record time. I was secretly hoping they wouldn't be able to pull it off so fast; the sting of rejection was still fresh in my mind. After all, it was only a few months ago that Lucas left me in Montauk on Fourth of July weekend without a word and has barely spoken to me since. I'm not saying I was innocent in the whole fiasco, but I really thought we were

3

getting a second chance, only to be punched in the gut by disappointment. I'm not going to lie: I've been dreading the whole thing since the night Jake and Ashley told me their great idea to elope to Mexico. Which was the day after they got engaged, which was only four months after they started dating. When they first told me the news, I immediately asked Ash if she was pregnant. Wouldn't that be everyone's first reaction? After all, it had only been four months! Who gets engaged after only four months?

But no, they swore there was no baby and they just didn't want to spend a year planning a big wedding. They would much rather have an intimate ceremony somewhere beautiful, and as soon as possible. What was the point of waiting if they were so sure about each other? They kept the guest list small, including a handful of close friends, our parents, myself as maid of honor, and obviously Jake's two best friends from childhood, Alex and Lucas, as groomsmen. Despite my reluctance to attend, I obviously wouldn't miss it, so all I can do is power through with a smile on my face and pretend like everything is fine.

Luckily the customs line has picked up, as do my hopes, just to be dashed again when I see the actual system at play here. When it's their turn, people press a button which prompts either a red or green light from what appears to be a large stoplight hanging overhead. Green, you pass through. Red, the Mexican Federales, or whoever the hell are running this show, stop and search your luggage. There doesn't seem to be any deciding factor except pure, dumb luck.

I look around at my fellow travelers to see if they think this is as ridiculous as I do. I see some surprised faces, but mostly people look weary, hot and sweaty. I can't believe this is the process to get into this country. I mentally run down the list of crap in my luggage in case I get a red light and my belongings are strewn all over the place in front of all these people like the poor guy it's happening to right now. His face is beet red and I feel so bad for him that I have to avert my eyes. I once watched an episode of a reality show where a woman was stopped at customs, and after rummaging through her luggage the customs officer found three large dildos. I almost turned the show off; the third-party embarrassment was more than I could handle. I say a silent prayer of gratitude that I didn't pack any dildos on this trip. However, my best lace lingerie is in there, just in case I happen to meet a hot, single man in the next few days. I snort to myself. Ash probably has every minute of the next three days accounted for, never mind any time for me to seduce a man. Also, I know everyone attending this wedding, and none are available or eligible. Even Alex has recently started dating some chick he met at the gym. So unless there's a random single guy at this super-romantic, adults-only resort in Cozumel, the chances of any male seeing my sexiest lingerie are slim to none.

I'm snapped back from my dream of seducing a hot Mexican bachelor when one of the officers signals that it's my turn to press the button. My heart starts pounding in my ears; with my luck, this thing will flash red and a siren will start blaring. My fear must be emanating from my body in waves since the middle-aged woman standing behind me in line gives me a sympathetic smile and nod of encouragement. I offer a small smile back, gather my nerve and reach out to press the button.

Green! *Yes!*

The relief in the air is palpable. I literally wipe the

sweat from my brow and forge through. Next up is a little booth where the officer takes my passport and asks my reason for traveling.

I must be temporarily possessed, because my mouth opens and words start flying out. "Hi, I'm Lila Turner. I'm here for my brother's wedding. Older brother. He's older, just so you know. By two years. Even though he's marrying my best friend. Who's my age. *And* I'm like, the only single one going. Because *his* best friend dumped me four months ago. If you can call leaving me at the beach without so much as a goodbye and totally ghosting me afterward actually dumping me." *Oh my God Lila, stop talking. Stop talking now!* I slap my hand over my mouth just in case it wants to keep disobeying my brain.

The officer gives me a blank stare, hands me back my stamped passport, and yells, "Next!" as if he didn't hear a word I said.

I wonder how many crazy answers he gets to that question. I can't be the first to lay my life story on him, I think as I drag my roller behind me and out the front door.

The Mexican sun blinds me again, and in the second I blink, I'm hit with a bear hug and a shriek, completely catching me off guard and almost knocking me off my feet. I smile to myself; I'd know that shriek anywhere.

"Ash, whoa," I say, trying to calm the excited blonde jumping up and down in front of me.

"Ahhhhh, I'm getting *married*! Thank God you're here. What took you so long? I need my maid of honor, the mothers are seriously stressing me out," she says, grabbing my hand. She leads me to where my brother is double-parked in a rental Jeep Wrangler with no doors.

He hops out, grabs my roller suitcase and leans in for

a hug. "This is all you packed? Wow, impressive. You should see Ash's three huge suitcases. She left me half of one for my own stuff." His eyes twinkle as he teases her.

She slaps his shoulder affectionately.

I reach into my carry-on and pull out the dress-up tiara I saved from the bachelorette party and put it on her head.

She beams at me. "I can't believe you brought this. You're amazing." She turns to the taxi line on the sidewalk and shouts, "*It's my wedding!*" Startling the line of passengers waiting for their transportation.

Jake and I both laugh as we climb into the Jeep.

"So our moms are being our moms?" I ask, raising my brows as my eyes connect with Jake's in the rearview mirror.

"You know them. Always trying to be in control of everything," he answers with a shrug.

Both of them took over the wedding planning with fervor immediately after they were told of the Mexico idea. They tried to organize everything, even the tiniest little details.

"Mom offered to write my speech for me," I say with a snort.

Jake and Ash turn to look at each other, lips pressed together, holding in their laughter. "Sounds about right," my brother says, nodding at me in the mirror.

"I think they're both forgetting it's our wedding and not a second chance to redo their own," Ash says, looking back at me and rolling her eyes.

"How's the speech coming, anyway?" Jake asks. "Do you know what you're going to say yet?"

Ash's ears perk up and she turns around to look at me from the front seat, eyes wide with anticipation.

I shake my head. "No, no. No sneak-peeks! You'll just have to wait and see on the big night." I try to smooth out my face, but anxiety whirls in my chest. I'm secretly terrified of giving this speech. Any type of public speaking is so not my jam, and in front of Lucas no less. Thankfully, I already have most of it memorized. I just pray my mind doesn't go blank when I'm up there in front of the whole party.

I subtly segue to more important topics at hand. "So when is Alex coming?" I ask, even though I already know the answer. Alex is Jake's other best friend, and like a second brother to me. And even though I could really use his calming presence right now, I'm trying to stealthily fish for info on when the other groomsman is actually arriving. The one I'm both dreading and longing to see.

"He gets in later tonight. He couldn't take the day off work," my brother says, not offering any additional info.

Realizing I'm not going to get the answers I'm looking for, I let it go and we talk about wedding details the rest of the way to the hotel. My mind wanders as they break down the itinerary for the next few days, which apparently includes a super-romantic luau right on the beach with tiki torches and a mariachi band.

I'm not sure when this crush on Lucas developed, really. All I know is that for as long as I can remember, I've had it. Like a birthmark or a mole that you carry with you through life, never really knowing if you were born with it or if one day it just appeared. The three of them have been inseparable since the first day of kindergarten—my brother Jake, Alex and Lucas. Alex Cooper was the chubby kid with freckles and an easy smile that could light up a room. Lucas Hayes, the strong, silent type—not brooding exactly, but not bubbly, either. The typical tall, dark and handsome hero in every movie. And Jake, my brother, the balance between the two—tall and lanky with dark-brown hair and matching eyes, like my own. Somehow their personalities meshed well from the get-go, and they formed an easy friendship solidified by their commitment to youth hockey.

Growing up across the street, Alex was a fixture in our house as far back as I can remember. He has three sisters and I guess felt overwhelmed in his own full house, so always came over to ours. Even though he has real sisters of his own, he always made me feel like his favorite—making it a point to include me and inviting me to play whatever silly game they cooked up. If I was ever having a bad day, or something happened at school to upset me, he'd be there as a shoulder to lean on. Always asking how I was and interested in my life.

Don't get me wrong, I worshipped my brother when we were kids—but Alex and I have a different bond. Not like Jake was ever bothered by it; I think he was actually relieved that someone else was taking over his brotherly responsibilities. Growing up, Jake and I were close in that "I only have one sibling" kind of way, where you had to be because it's convenient when there's nobody else around to play with. Being only two years apart, I was the annoying little sister, but could also pass for a satisfactory playmate in the direst of circumstances.

Lucas was a different story. He was the only child of parents who got divorced when he was just a baby, and his mom, a working single parent, was hardly ever around. Left to his own devices from a young age, he was forced to grow up faster than the rest of us. The lack of a big support system resulted in a limited trust in those around him, and Lucas put up a guard that was written all over his face. He never let this guard down easily, and certainly not for just anyone. You had to really build trust with him before he warmed to you. Lucas was also extremely easy on the eyes, which he never seemed comfortable with. It was like the older he got, the hotter he got, and the more his distrust in people grew. In high school, this gave him a bad-boy air that lured in the girls like you can't even imagine. Let me tell you, there is nothing sexier than a standoffish, hot, teenage athlete.

I'm ripped back from my trip down memory lane as Jake makes a sharp turn onto a narrow street. I steady myself in my seat and watch as the road eventually opens up into a wider drive and the hotel grounds come into view. We pass a large fountain with two stone frogs in the center spitting water at each other, and drive up to a beautiful glass building with a circular driveway. Whoa, it's absolutely stunning. This is not your usual large vacation resort, but rather a small boutique hotel, and one of the only available on such short notice. However, it doesn't skimp on the grandeur. The grounds are exquisitely manicured with tropical trees and bright, colorful flowers everywhere, and the staff are lined up outside, awaiting guest arrivals, decked out in impeccably tailored uniforms. The whole front entrance is floor-to-ceiling glass, so you can see straight through to the pool and beach on the other side. I'm speechless as I take in my surroundings.

The valet comes around and helps me out of the back.

"Beautiful, right?" Ash asks me when she sees my face.

I can only nod, my eyes huge as I follow them through the glass sliding doors and into the marble lobby.

My brother hands me my roller and directs me to the front desk to check in and get my room key. "Meet us at the bar when you're all checked in. We'll be outside—you can't miss it." He points over my shoulder to another set of sliding glass doors leading to the back of the hotel that open onto an enormous patio with a bar on one side and a lounge area with tables, chairs and couches for guests to relax on the other.

In the middle is a stone path leading past an infinity pool—which looks like it goes straight into the ocean—and on down to the beach. This place is truly drop-dead gorgeous, and giving off serious honeymoon vibes. There are couples everywhere I look—in front of me, making googly eyes at each other; in the lobby, waiting to check in; another enjoying cocktails on a couch in the outside lounge; and one more folded over each other on a sunbed out by the pool. I sigh to myself and try to bite back the familiar sting of the reality of my current single status, which seems especially aggressive in a place so beautiful and made to celebrate romance. Oh well, I hope I get at least an hour to relax on one of those sunbeds myself; maybe I can pretend I'm on my own honeymoon and my husband is inside taking a nap. I snort at my own ridiculousness as I wait in line to check in.

When it's my turn, the attendant rushes around the counter to grab my suitcase and assures me a porter will bring it up to my room. He gives me my room key and directions to the elevator bank down the hall, and sends me on my way with a wink.

I take the elevator up to my floor, marveling at the lavishness of it all. Jesus Christ, this must have cost a fortune. Thank God they decided to elope with a limited number of people, I think as I fumble with my room key.

I open the door to a small but beautifully decorated room with a king bed and a tiny balcony overlooking the ocean. I go straight to the balcony, throw open the doors and step outside to the landing, sipping in the salty ocean air. The water is an exquisite turquoise blue and I close my eyes, take a deep breath and listen to the waves. I leave the door open and walk back into the room, sit on the bed and kick off my shoes. I breathe in and out, slowly counting my breaths just like my therapist taught me, trying to calm my nerves and think back on the events of my life and how exactly I wound up here.

CHAPTER 2

SUMMER 2005

I 'm in the backyard, trying to get a jump on my sixth-grade reading list when I'm rudely interrupted by my brother, Alex and Lucas. I roll my eyes when I realize what they're hollering at each other about—who can climb the big oak tree the fastest. As they advance toward my quiet studying spot under said oak, I realize Tom Sawyer and his adventures will have to wait, since it looks like this contest is happening right now. My heart starts to race as Lucas draws near. It's like my body has a mind of its own and starts to go haywire whenever he's close. I don't really understand it, but there's no denying this fluttery feeling in my stomach every time he's around me.

I abandon my book on the grass and focus my attention on the show before me. Alex scrambles up the tree in record time, with Lucas not too far behind. It takes Jake a little longer, and I giggle along when the other two tease him for being slow.

Jake doesn't like that too much. "Let's see you try and beat me," my brother snaps at me with a scowl on his face.

This pisses me off, and I gladly accept the challenge. I get up, glaring at him, and brush off my pants as I look up at the massive tree before me. Panic shoots down my spine as I realize I may have bitten off more than I can chew here.

The boys must see the hesitation on my face. Jake snickers, and Alex, the sweetheart that he is, tries to bail me out. "Ignore him, Lila," he says, looking nervous as nods in Jake's direction. "He's just mad that he's the slowest. You don't have to do it."

I consider this for a second and glance over at Lucas.

His jaw is clenched and his brow is furrowed, but he doesn't say a word. The fact that he cares gives me a rush, which just makes me all the more determined to prove myself to these boys.

I step onto the first branch easily, and continue to climb branch by branch while they watch below in silence. I'm finally at the top, in record time no less, and smirk down at Jake, who's fuming. "Ha! I definitely beat your time," I whoop, a grin splitting my face in two.

"Whatever," he mumbles as he walks away, kicking at the grass with his sneakers.

With a shit-eating grin still plastered on my face, I start my descent. A rogue branch catches the loop on my jeans, throwing me off balance. My foot misses the next branch and I fall back, catapulting toward the ground.

Crap. I squeeze my eyes shut, bracing for impact, when all of a sudden I feel arms around me. My eyes fly open and meet Lucas's, his face inches from my own, right before we both hit the ground.

"Holy shit!" Alex runs over to us. "Are you guys okay?" Fear laces his voice.

I lift my head to see Lucas sprawled on the grass next

to me as Alex leans down, reaching out to me to see if I'm okay. I roll away from him and crawl over to Lucas, who's lying still with his eyes closed. Dread pools in my belly that he might be dead, and I poke his arm harder than intended.

"Ouch!" he yelps as his eyes fly open and he grabs his arm.

"Ohthankgod," I breathe out and collapse back on the grass.

He hoists himself up to sitting and stares down at me.

I stare back at him. "You caught me," I say in disbelief.

"Yeah." He nods, like that was the obvious thing to do.

I don't know what to say. Tears prick my eyes as the reality of Lucas saving my life hits me.

"I told you not to climb the tree, Lila!" Alex yells at me, pulling me back to the moment.

"Sorry, sorry," I mutter, swatting his hands away as he pokes and prods me, checking if I'm hurt. I look over at Lucas's pinched face; he looks like he's the one in pain. "Lucas, are you really okay?" I ask. I fell down pretty hard right on top of him.

"Yeah, yeah. I'm fine," he says. "Are you sure you're okay?" he asks, his eyes assessing me.

"I'm fine. You broke my fall...Thanks." I smile at him.

"It was nothing." He hoists himself to his feet. I see him wince as he puts weight on his leg. He notices me watching him and tries to hide it, turning his back to me.

"Wait, you're not fine! You're hurt!" I shriek as my panic rises again, now really concerned I may have broken this boy.

He puts his hand against the tree for support, but shakes his head at me. "No, no, I'm fine."

I'm not buying it. "Here, sit down," I say as I try to

guide him back to the ground. "Go get him ice," I bark at Alex while he watches in concern.

His eyes widen in alarm and he turns and runs into the house.

I crouch next to Lucas on the grass. "Where does it hurt?" I start rolling up the leg of his jeans.

"Really, it's okay, Lila. I'm fine. It's probably just a bruise. No big deal," he tries to assure me.

I keep rolling up his pant leg and see the blood trickling from a scrape on his shin. I immediately freak out, my thoughts going straight to the worst-case scenario: my stupid bravado cost Lucas his leg. "You're bleeding!" I accuse him like it's his fault, and it wasn't me who just fell out of a tree, hitting him like a ton of bricks while he tried to save me from hurting myself.

He shrugs a shoulder at me. "It's just a little blood, I'm fine."

I unzip my hoodie and rip it off. I frantically start wrapping a sleeve around his leg to stop the bleeding.

He laughs at my makeshift tourniquet. He puts a hand on mine; his large hand is warm and comforting. "I'll survive, I promise." He smiles at me, and the anxiety I feel contorting my face starts to subside.

I catch the humor in his twinkling eyes and I sit back on the grass, realizing I'm overreacting as a laugh escapes my own lips.

"You'd be a good nurse one day." He squeezes my hand, still grinning at me. Our eyes catch as I grin back, still feeling my shoulders ease with the relief that he's not seriously injured. Time slows as our gaze locks, and we continue to smile at one another, neither one breaking eye contact. The fluttery feeling inside me intensifies as time stretches. Maybe this boy actually sees me for who I am and not the annoying little sister my brother makes me out to be? Lucas's throat bobs as he swallows, and I notice the tiniest flecks of yellow in his green eyes.

The moment is broken when Alex and Jake come running out of the house yelling that they have ice. After assuring them he's fine, Lucas gets up and leads them back into the house, leaving me alone on the grass.

The smile lingers on my face long after they're gone.

Chapter 3

"O uch!" I yelp as my bra strap snaps against my left shoulder. I turn around and look at the culprit. Ugh—Mark, one of my brother's hockey teammates and constant pain in my ass, stands right behind me. He's made it his life's mission to torment me ever since elementary school.

I narrow my eyes at him. "Grow up, Mark."

He snickers at me, then knocks his shoulder into mine, causing my notebook to fly out of my hands and hit the floor. Damnit.

I bend down to retrieve it while rubbing my shoulder. I just so happen to be sunburnt from the last weekend of summer vacation, so my skin is particularly sensitive. As I lean down, my bag opens and the rest of my books fall out. *Shit.* I close my eyes and let out a sigh, my shoulders slumping in frustration. The first day of high school—joy.

"Let me help you." A familiar voice startles me and my eyes fly open. Lucas bends down and grabs the books before I can. His brows are furrowed in concern, softening the edge to his otherwise impenetrable demeanor. "Are you okay?" he asks.

Heat floods my insides. Of course Lucas has to see me like this on my first day of high school. I feel my cheeks burn and look away. "Yeah, yeah. I'm fine," I assure him as I take the books from his outstretched hand. I stand and open my locker, shoving the books inside.

He reaches over my shoulder, tucks a book that I must have missed next to the others and turns around to face Mark. "Leave her alone, will you? It's her first day for God's sake."

Mark scoffs back at him. "I'm just messing with her. All in good fun. Relax, Luke." He backs away with his hands up and takes off down the hall.

"Ignore him. His mind is obviously stuck back in first grade. He has no idea how to talk to women," Lucas says, shaking his head as he opens his own locker, which appears to be right next to mine.

My eyes widen in surprise. "That's your locker?" I blurt out, pointing to it.

"Yup. Looks like we're neighbors," he says with a faint smile on his lips.

Wow, I can't believe I won the locker lottery. I never win anything. In middle school my locker was right next to the boys' bathroom. I had to hold my breath every time I needed to swap out my books.

I try to hide my considerable delight. "Cool." I nod. *Cool?* Oh God, rewind! Can't I think of anything better? Lucas is actually talking to me in public here. And he practically referred to me as a woman. "Um, thanks for the help back there," I add meekly, wincing at how small my voice sounds.

His eyes flash with amusement. "No problem." He

shuts his locker. "Have a good day, Lila. Try to stay out of trouble." He winks at me as he saunters off to class.

Gathering myself, I walk to my own first-period class and take a seat at the empty desk next to Ashley—the only other person I've voiced my crush on Lucas to.

I put my bag down and turn to face her, unable to contain my grin. "Lucas's locker is next to mine." I wiggle my brows up and down.

She smirks and eyes me with approval. "Wow, aren't you lucky. Mine is next to that slimeball, Mark."

I wrinkle my nose and laugh at this. "Yeah, Lucas actually came to my rescue after said slimeball assaulted me in the hall just now."

"Wow, a rescue by your very own knight in shining armor on the first day, *and* before first period too! Look at you, crushing high school already." She playfully slaps my arm.

"I know, crazy right?" I shake my head while trying to control my laughter.

She agrees, still grinning. "High school is a whole new world."

I hate high school. It's only lunch and my head is so crammed with information that I actually have a migraine. The amount of homework I have already is seriously concerning. If day one is any indication of how this year is going to be, there goes my social life.

I'm complaining about all of this to Ash during lunch when my brother and his friends walk into the cafeteria, strutting to an empty table wearing their varsity hockey jackets, being loud and attracting attention, as usual.

They tend to draw eyes to themselves, especially those of the female sex.

Lucas follows behind the group, his face unreadable as he takes a seat at the end of the table. My breath catches as I notice how hot he looks today. To say he's extremely easy on the eyes is an understatement. His tall, broad-shouldered frame seems to be getting even more muscular each day. His light-brown hair is freshly shorn into his signature buzz cut, and his piercing green eyes perfectly set off the lingering summer glow from his olive skin.

Those eyes catch mine from across the room and his lips turn up in a small smile.

I smile back, barely listening to Ash relay her morning to me, when our gaze is broken as Chloe Bailey sits down right on Lucas's lap. I blink a couple of times to make sure my eyes aren't playing tricks on me.

"Um, Lila? Your jaw is literally on the floor." Ash follows my line of sight. "Huh, interesting," she says as she registers what has me ruffled.

"What the hell?" I whisper-shout at Ash. "I didn't know they were a thing."

"Well, she is captain of the cheerleading squad. You can hardly be surprised."

I gape at her, silently imploring a more detailed explanation for what's going down across the room.

"What? Pretty, athletic people attract other pretty, athletic people." She shrugs like this should be common knowledge to me. I guess she does have a point there. This is just another reminder of how out of my league Lucas is anyway.

I sigh and finish my peanut butter and jelly sandwich, calculating the minutes until this day will finally be over.

Alex spots us and comes over to our table. "How's the first day going?" he asks as he takes a seat. He grabs a pretzel from the open bag in front of me and pops it into his mouth. I give him a pained expression. "Oof. That bad, huh?" He cocks his head in sympathy.

"Don't mind her, she'll be fine," Ash pipes in, offering him her bag of chips. He takes them from her with a grunt of thanks. She's used to the insatiable hunger of my brother and his friends; teenage males have bottomless pits for stomachs.

"What's happening over there?" I gesture in the direction of his table across the room.

His eyes follow to where my finger is pointing. "What?" He genuinely looks confused at first, then I see the realization dawn in his eyes. "Oh, Luke and Chloe?" He shrugs and shoves a handful of chips in his mouth. "Who knows, she's constantly flitting around him. They're on and off every other day."

I feel my insides squeeze. "Really? Seriously? Is this a new thing?" I try to sound nonchalant, but I'm failing.

Alex eyes me over the bag of chips. Ash tries to hide her smile behind the apple she's nibbling on.

"What? I'm just asking," I say, giving him my best I-don't-care look.

"Mhmm." He ignores my question and gets up from his seat. "Hang in there ducklings, only a few hours left," he says as he ruffles my hair and walks back to the popular table.

Ash lets her laugh break free. "Smooth," she says to me.

I groan and lean my head down to rest on my arm. "Can't this day just be over already?"

CHAPTER 4

FALL 2009

I'm waiting outside the school, using my books as a shield against the rain, and silently curse out my brother in my head. He's at least twenty minutes late picking me up and I could scream. I call his cell for the tenth time with no luck, so I try Alex again too. Voicemail. I stifle a scream and look down at my clothes; I'm completely soaked. After a whole year of picking me up at the same time every day, you would think they would be on time.

I try to find shelter under the overhang, but the wind makes my attempt futile. My hopes lift when I see a car pulling out of the lot, only to fall again when I realize it's not Jake's car. *Where the hell is he?* As the car creeps closer, I realize it's Lucas.

He stops when he spots me rolls down the window. "Lila? Do you need a ride? Get in." He leans over to unlock the door for me.

I hesitate and look down at my clothes. I look like a wet rat, but I really need a ride home. I open the door and climb in, soaking his front seat. "I'm so sorry." I try to wipe up the moisture with my wet jacket, only making it worse. I sigh and lean back in the seat. "Jake was supposed to pick me up; he and Alex aren't answering my calls, and I've been waiting forever." Annoyance sharpens my words.

"Don't worry about it. They got held up at practice—Coach caught them dicking around and made them stay late to do extra drills. I can drive you home, no problem."

He reaches over me to open the glove compartment and hands me some napkins. I get a whiff of him when he leans over, and my teenage hormones skyrocket. He smells amazing—freshly showered from practice, his hair still a little wet. I try not to lean in and inhale like a weirdo. *Pull it together, Lila.*

He helps me dry off my books, then leans back over to drop the wet napkins on the floor at my feet. His hand brushes my leg as he leans back up. The butterflies in my stomach go wild.

"Are you sure you don't mind?" I'm frantically trying to dry myself off before I ruin the leather of his front seat.

His eyes shine in amusement as he watches me flail around. "Of course not." He puts the car in gear and starts driving.

My heartbeat accelerates as the seconds pass in silence. He's never been much of a talker, and I rack my brain for something to say. This is so awkward. *Lila, just say something, anything!*

"So are you still dating Chloe?" I blurt out, then instantly cringe. That's what I come up with? Literally anything would have been better after the tumultuous last year of them breaking up and getting back together every other week. I spent my whole first year of high school on the Lucas-and-Chloe drama train.

He looks surprised by my question. "Why would you think that?" he asks, his brows furrowed.

"Oh, I don't know. I didn't see you that much this summer. Not that I really noticed, it wasn't like I was stalking you. I don't care or anything. No big deal, it's cool." The words catapult out of my mouth. *Oh my God, am I having a stroke? Stop talking!*

He laughs and looks at me sideways. I wince and shrink back into my seat, wishing the car would swallow me whole.

"No, definitely not back together," he says with a definitive shake of his head. "What about you? Now that you have a year of high school under your belt, I bet all the guys are drooling over you."

What? Why would he think that? I scoff at him. "Oh yeah, just drooling. Like five guys asked me out this weekend alone."

His eyes cut to me fast. "Seriously?" He asks, alarmed.

"Um, no." I give him a coy look.

He smiles and shakes his head. "Don't act like it's such a crazy idea. You should see how guys look at you."

My jaw drops in disbelief. Is he serious? Nobody ever looks at me. They look at Ash, the hot blonde. They may skim over me, the petite brunette, but their eyes always land on her.

"You'll see one day," he says to me. "Jake, Alex and I... we have our work cut out for us."

"What's that supposed to mean?" I wrinkle my nose at him.

"You'll be breaking hearts in no time," he says with a nod of his head.

I stifle an eye roll. He's crazy. "And what about you?" I ask. "Obviously you see how all the girls follow you around. *Like Chloe*."

He smirks at me. "Do I detect jealousy?"

I feel my face heat up. "No, no, I'm just saying," I sputter. "Just, glass houses and all," I say and glance out the window.

He finally pulls up to my house. This conversation has made the vibe in the car even more awkward. He surprises me when he puts the car in park and turns to face me. "Just be careful. Not all guys have the best intentions, especially at our age." His eyes bore into mine.

I squirm in my seat. "Thanks for the advice." I reach down and grab my bag. "And the ride," I add as I open the door to get out.

"Lila, wait." He reaches over and grabs my hand.

I turn back, startled by the physical contact. "Yeah?"

He looks at me, confusion fogging his features like he is struggling to find his words. We stare at each other for a good minute, neither of us speaking, my hand in his. I watch his piercing green eyes trail down my face to my lips and back up to lock with mine, sending my heart pounding. I'm paralyzed in this moment, unable to look away from his penetrating gaze.

All of a sudden, realization dawns in his eyes and he drops my hand and looks away. "Nothing. Never mind. See you at school." He scrubs a hand down his face and stares straight ahead, not looking back at me. He puts the car in drive and I take that as my cue to exit.

I stand in the street under the pouring rain, staring

after him as he drives away, wondering what the hell just happened.

The next day, I feel a slap on my ass while I'm trying to get to my third-period Spanish class. Annoyed, I turn around to see Mark grinning from ear to ear. Jesus, it never ends with this guy.

"What's up, Lila?" He puts an arm around my shoulder and ruffles my hair.

I inwardly cringe, but at least he's not knocking my books to the ground anymore. "Glad to see you graduated from snapping my bra strap." I elbow him in the ribs.

"Ouch! Okay, okay!" He steps back with his hands out in surrender. "You better be coming to John's party Friday night!" he says, wiggling his eyebrows as he backs off down the hall.

"Yeah right, I'm sure Jake will just love that," I mutter, more to myself than him. I turn into the classroom for Spanish, the only class that Ash and I share this year, and sit next to her in our row. I grunt a hello while chewing on the end of my pen, mentally working out how to get Jake to agree to let us go to this party. John is also on the hockey team and Jake is a regular at his famous parties.

It's been the talk of the school for days and I really want to go, but I just don't think it's happening.

Ash must notice something is up by my face. "What's that look for?" Being friends for over ten years, she can read me like a book.

"Well, you know that party everyone's been talking about all week? Apparently we've just been invited."

Her jaw drops and she looks like she might fall out of her chair. "We are *so* going." I see the wheels start to turn in her head with the logistics of a night out: outfits, makeup, etc.

"I thought you might say that," I say, removing the pen from my mouth and pointing it at her. "But not sure how thrilled Jake will be about it."

Ash cocks her head as she considers this, knowing it's probably true. Her eyes light up. "You should ask Alex!" She reaches out to grab my wrist. "Maybe he'll agree to take us? He doesn't mind so much when we tag along." She looks so optimistic, I try not to let my skepticism kill the hope in her eyes.

She's not wrong; Alex sometimes will bring us out, but more like to the mall or the movies, not exactly a senior party on a Friday night. I guess now that we have a year of high school behind us, it's less weird for us all to hang out. But still, this doesn't mean Jake necessarily loves it when we do. Although, we're finally past the awkward middle-school age where it's not really acceptable to hang with your baby sister.

The one thing he and Alex both agree on is being super protective of me when it comes to guys. They're not thrilled with the idea of me dating anybody, my age or not. Not that they've ever really had to worry about it before. My all-consuming crush on Lucas kind of eliminates my interest in anybody else. I've only ever had eyes for him, who is totally off-limits, obviously. Ash has dragged me along on a few double dates, but I've only agreed to go to be a good wing-woman, not because I've actually liked any of the guys.

I've tried not to be so obvious about my crush on Lucas, especially in front of Jake, but I think everyone probably knows about it. Mercifully, nobody has ever voiced any comments on the subject. Nobody other than Ash, that is. Besides the fact that Lucas is Jake and Alex's best friend, there is our age difference to consider. Plus, we run in different social circles, him being a hot, popular jock and all.

I never thought he would be interested in me, but after the other day in the car, I've been wondering if maybe I was wrong. Did that lingering look really happen, or was it a figment of my imagination? I've always believed this crush lived solely in my head, some epic, unrequited love story that just plays on a loop for my eyes only. But now I'm starting to think that maybe he feels something, too. Maybe it's not such a far-fetched, impossible dream after all.

I get my chance to broach the subject with Alex later that day while he's giving me driving lessons in the middle school parking lot. I'm late getting my license because I have so many people to drive me around, so I haven't felt the urgency to take the test yet. Jake, Alex and Ash all have cars of their own, plus we live in a small town that's pretty walkable if the three of them or my parents aren't around.

"Brake, Lila!" Alex yells at me for the tenth time. I apparently have a heavy foot.

"Sorry! Jeez, driving is stressful. How do you guys do this all the time?" I really suck at this. My feet can't seem to understand the difference between the two pedals and it's maddening. More so for the passenger, which Alex has graciously agreed to be on more than one occasion.

My parents are busy at work, and Jake refuses to give me lessons, so Alex, being the sweetheart he is, has taken on the job.

"It's okay, you just need some more practice. But for the millionth time, can you please *not* drive with two feet? It will make it so much easier, I promise." He's tried to convince me of this numerous times, to no avail.

"Okay, okay, I'll try!" I say as I pull the car over. *It's now or never.* "So, I heard there's a party at John's on Friday..." I say as I give him my best puppy dog eyes.

"Yeah?" He raises a brow, knowing where this is going.

My fingers grip the wheel. "Maybe Ash and I can come out with you guys?"

His eyes light up with amusement. "Did you ask Jake already?"

I grimace. "You know Jake hates to be seen with his little sister."

"Oh come on, that's not true," he scoffs.

"Yes it is. He's not exactly begging me to hang out. Look at you here right now teaching me to drive instead of him. He refuses to even give me one driving lesson."

He looks at me sympathetically. "It's not that he doesn't want you around, he's just protective of you. We all are. Honestly, it's better for you to be stuck with me anyway—he's definitely not as patient as I am." He laughs and nudges my shoulder. "He'd probably rip off one of your feet at this point."

"Ha-ha." I roll my eyes at him. "So, does that mean you'll take us?" I try again.

He sighs. "Yes, fine. I'll talk to Jake," he assures me. "Now hop out. Let me show you how this is done." He unbuckles his seatbelt and opens the door.

I unbuckle my own belt and climb over the middle to the passenger seat, trying to hide my smile. I feel a rush of excitement in my chest; I can't wait to call Ash as soon as I get home and tell her to start planning our outfits for this party.

CHAPTER 5

After school on Friday, Ashley and I go back to my house and spend two hours in my room getting ready.

"Did you shave your legs?" she asks me with a suggestive smile.

"Umm, no?" I pause to think about it for a second. "Should I? You think there's a chance Lucas will take my pants off tonight?" I ask her, my voice rising in alarm. I figured we were just going to hang out with them as a group. I never really considered that tonight could possibly be the night that Lucas would see me naked.

Her face splits into a grin, and I realize she's teasing me. "Better to be prepared just in case, right?" She shrugs.

"Ash!" I slap her on the shoulder. "I'm nervous enough as it is."

"Oh stop, it's gonna be fun! How excited are you to finally hang out with Lucas though?"

"Well, let's not get ahead of ourselves here. What if he pretends not to even know us?" I wince at the thought. This idea has been running through my head all day. I have no idea what he's like at parties. More importantly, I have no idea what he'll be like *with me*. Will he ignore me and treat me like his friend's annoying little sister, or will he hang out with me and not care about being seen talking to a sophomore?

"No, he would never. We've been hanging out with these guys our whole lives, just in another setting. How different can a senior party be? Plus, we have Alex. He won't ditch us," she says definitively.

She is right about that—I'm confident Alex at least will stick with us tonight. Jake, on the other hand, wasn't so thrilled with the idea of us going. But Lucas is a wild card; he could go either way.

"I just don't want to get my hopes up. I've held Lucas up on a pedestal forever, and I'm nervous that the real-life version will smash my dream version of him," I admit.

Ash nods. "I get it—it would be kind of devastating if he was a horrible kisser or his dick curved to the left." She raises a brow at me, and we both burst out laughing. Even joking about Lucas's penis makes me start to sweat.

After we spend twenty minutes grooming ourselves to *Playboy* pin-up perfection, Ashley is satisfied. She is truly talented with a curling iron—my brown hair falls in perfect waves down my back, and she has shaded, lined and mascaraed my eyes to make them pop. "Wow," I say, admiring her handiwork in the mirror. "We look pretty amazing."

She adds a little more blush to her own cheeks, nodding in agreement. Her long blonde hair is styled similarly to my own, and her complexion glows thanks to her endless collection of highlighters, blush and bronzer.

"We do, indeed. Senior boys, eat your hearts out!" She winks at me.

At least one of us is optimistic about tonight—my insides feel like a puddle of goo. I'm praying her confidence will rub off on me in the car.

Alex yells upstairs for us to get a move on.

Ash makes one last adjustment to my hair, and we grab our stuff and head out the door.

We walk into John's house and the party is already well underway. Music is blasting, and there are people everywhere—mostly people from school, but also some I've never seen before. There's a keg in the kitchen and a beer-pong table set up on the enclosed porch.

John comes over to greet the guys and Jake disappears into the fray without a second glance. So much for any hand-holding from him. He barely said two words to us in the car, clearly miffed we tagged along tonight. Alex tells us to have fun, but not too much fun, as he promised my parents he would get us home in one piece by curfew. Which means "do not get sloppy." Fine by me. Being the control freak that I am, I tend to slow down once I start to get too tipsy anyway. My plan tonight is to pace myself. Ashley, on the other hand, could benefit from someone keeping an eye on her. She has a wild streak that is fueled by alcohol.

John pours us each a beer from the keg and we head onto the porch where a beer-pong game is just ending.

Mark excitedly calls next game. "Ash, Lila, get over here!" he says, beckoning us over to the table.

"How about you and Ash against me and Lila?" Lucas offers.

My face grows hot as I try to hide my smile while Ash voices her agreement. I'm keenly aware of Lucas's physical proximity as we set up our cups. I try to focus on Mark teasing Ash at the other end of the table.

"You better make some of these," Lucas says to me with a glint in his eye. "Don't make me drink all of these beers myself."

I lift an eyebrow. "Excuse me, I am a beer-pong champion. You just watch and learn," I say with bravado. This game is actually one I am somehow talented at.

"We'll just see about that."

I can't control my smile as he holds my gaze for a beat.

"Alright, look alive people." Ash claps at us from across the room, trying to get our attention to start the game.

They start off strong with Mark getting two cups in a row, but then lose momentum as Ashley misses her shots.

Our turn. I make my first cup, and I throw my hands up and do a little curtsy.

Ashley rolls her eyes. "Ugh, she always makes her first cup! She's so good, it's not fair."

I open my mouth in mock horror, call her a sore loser and shoot again. I make another cup and stick my tongue out at her this time.

She returns the gesture, and we both crack up laughing.

I feel Lucas staring at me, so I turn to face him. "What?" I give him a shrug. "I did tell you I was good at this," I say with a smirk.

He looks at me in disbelief. "Wow. Glad I picked you for my team, then," he says, eyes twinkling at me.

Lucas sinks his next two cups, then I follow suit, and the game pretty much keeps going in that direction. My body buzzes with excitement. Lucas and I yell and high five after every cup. I'm having so much fun, and it seems like he is too. Before I know it, we're down to the last cup. Mark and Ash on the other hand have only made four out of ten, so there's quite a lot of beer still in front of us. I'm not even tipsy yet, but they're looking a bit glassy-eyed. I laugh as Ashley sways into Mark for the third time as she misses another shot.

"Okay, last cup. Don't choke now," I tease Lucas.

"Please," he scoffs back at me. "I can make this with my eyes closed." He holds my gaze as he raises his arm and shoots the ball. We hear the swoosh as the ball makes it into the cup, and simultaneously scream in triumph as I jump into his arms.

He catches me and spins me around. "Phew, so glad I made that last shot. I would've looked like a real ass if I missed," he says, as he puts me down.

"Hell yeah, you're lucky you made it! I would never have let you live that down." I beam at him.

"We make a pretty good team." He nods, smiling as big as I am.

Ashley and Mark are pouting at the other end of the table.

"Now come drink all these beers, losers!" I gesture at the cups in front of me.

Ash groans. "Ugh, you're not allowed to play anymore." She comes over still pouting and pours half the remaining cups into one and chugs it. "Rest is yours," she says to Mark. "I really have to pee." And she takes off in search of the bathroom, almost knocking Alex over on her way out of the room.

"Was that an invitation?" Mark asks us as he grabs his cups and follows her, eyebrows wiggling at us.

"Ew." I stifle an eye roll in his direction.

Lucas cracks a smile and shakes his head. "That dude will never grow up."

"Ooh, I got next game," Alex says as he sees all the empty cups on the table.

Lucas looks at me in question, and I shrug.

"You down for another?" I ask.

"Hell yeah!" he says.

"Who's gonna be your partner, Al?" I ask.

"I am," says my brother as he strolls into the room. He looks like he's already had a few himself. "Can't have my little sister having all the fun tonight." He gives me a pointed look.

Shit, Jake can be kind of a jerk when he's wasted. My palms start to sweat as my anxiety rises. I knew this night was too good to be true. A deep sense of dread settles in my gut while I watch my brother's pinched face as he racks up the cups.

Lucas and I rack and fill our own cups, and since we won the last game, we get to shoot first. Chills run down my spine as Lucas leans down and whispers, "You go first, killer," into my ear.

My face splits into a grin, then falters as I notice Jake frowning at us. *Okay, be cool, Lila.* I try to shake off the weird, threatening vibe.

I shoot the ball; it circles the rim of the cup twice, then lands in the beer. *Yes!* Lucas claps, Alex groans, Jake snatches up the cup and drinks the beer. I do a little dance in place before taking aim for my next shot. I eye my target cup and sink this one too. My arms shoot up. "Hell yeah, drink up!" I yell across the table, feeling myself.

"Jesus Lila, how did you get so good?" Alex grumbles. "Do you like practice at home or something?"

Lucas beams at me and tosses his arm over my shoulder. "She's something else, isn't she?"

I feel myself blush.

Alex goes to take the cup since it's his turn to drink the beer, but Jake grabs it out of his hand and pours it down his own throat. "Dude, what's with you?" Alex asks him, eyes narrowing.

Totally ignoring him, Jake cocks his head, still staring at Lucas. "Where's Chloe tonight, Luke?"

I feel Lucas stiffen beside me as I watch my brother continue to stare him down from the other end of the table. *Chloe?* Why would he care where Chloe is? He assured me the other day in the car they're not back together.

I look up to study his face, and see confusion furrowing his brow. I feel a tightness forming in my chest as my thoughts race a mile a minute. Are they really not over? Is my brother just drunk and being an asshole? What's happening right now?

Jake and Lucas continue to glower at each other, locked in some kind of silent battle I'm definitely not privy to. Lucas drops his arm from my shoulder. I immediately feel its absence, replaced by a cold sensation where it was resting.

I look to Alex for some kind of guidance as to what the hell is going on, but all I get is a shrug from him.

"Um, okay then," I say. "Not sure what the hell your problem is, Jake, but if you can stop being such a dick, maybe you want to shoot the fucking ball?" I glare at him.

He scowls at me and takes the shot. As it swishes into the cup, he walks out of the room.

"What the hell is his deal?" I say to no one in particular as I watch him disappear into the kitchen. I study Lucas's face for some answers, but he avoids my gaze. I turn to Alex, my question hanging in the air.

"It's nothing. Just ignore him," Alex says, giving me a small, reassuring smile. "Let's take a breather. We'll pick this up later." He pats me on the shoulder as he walks out of the room, leaving Lucas and me alone. Lucas still hasn't said a word since the Chloe comment. I don't care what Alex says, that definitely was not "nothing," and I want some answers.

I raise my eyebrows at him. "What was that about, Lucas?"

He tries to conceal the tightness in his jaw with a smile. "I really have no idea, I swear. I don't know why he would say that. I told you the other day, Chloe and I are over." He grabs my hand. "Let's get some air." He pulls me out the back door to the patio.

I'm so confused right now, but can only think about how Lucas is holding my hand. My thoughts swirl like a tornado in my head. Was Jake annoyed we were winning, or is Lucas lying to me about Chloe?

He leads me to an empty lounge chair by the pool and sits back, pulling me down into him. "I'm very impressed with your beer-pong skills," he says in my ear.

I'm stunned by the physical contact and can't seem to find my words.

He must sense my body tense up and mistakes it for irritation. He sighs. "Seriously, Lila, Jake is just being a drunk sore loser." He tugs on a strand of my hair and puts it behind my ear.

I try not to shiver. "Not what it looked like to me." I look back at him pointedly, and it takes everything in me to flick his hand away.

"Are you jealous?" he asks me, smirking. "How cute."

"Um, no." I elbow him in the ribs.

He grunts and grabs my arm, holding it still. He stares at me, the corners of his mouth curving upwards, and when I don't return the smile, he sighs again and scrubs a hand down his face. "Okay, okay. Guess he wasn't thrilled about us flirting," he breathes out.

This comment surprises me. "We were flirting?" I ask with a coy smile.

With an amused flick of an eyebrow, he says, "Maybe." He pulls me back into him, and I face forward and relax against his chest. His arms wrap around me and he rests his chin on my head. I don't even care about how pissed my brother is right now; all I can concentrate on is the buzzing through my body.

"This feels nice," Lucas whispers in my ear, his breath tickling my neck.

I guess the feeling is mutual. I'm trying not to smile like an idiot, but I'm finding it extremely difficult. I hum a sound of agreement.

"Really though, I can't believe how good at beer pong you are," he says with a laugh. "What other talents are you hiding?"

"Wouldn't you like to know," I say, and my eyes immediately go wide. Holy hell, did I actually just say that? My cheeks heat up, and I'm grateful he can't see my face right now.

His laughter rumbles against my back as he squeezes his arms tighter around me. "You are trouble."

I turn around to grin at him. His expression mirrors

mine, but in a split-second a flash of emotion moves across his face that I can't seem to put my finger on. Sadness? I cock my head slightly in a silent question.

"I can't believe we're graduating so soon," he finally says. "I just want time to slow down a bit. All of a sudden it feels like it's moving really fast." His brow furrows even more. "How could that have been our first game of beer pong?" he says softly.

I'm a bit taken aback. Lucas isn't exactly one to share his feelings. "I know, I'm really gonna miss you guys next year. All three of you are leaving me," I say, looking up at him. "Finally Ash and I can actually have some fun without the guard dogs around," I joke, trying to lighten the mood. If I really think about how my boys won't be around anymore, I'll start bawling my eyes out right now on this lounge chair.

That seems to do the trick. His lips turn up and he pokes his finger into my side. "Trouble," he repeats.

I lean back squirming, crushing him into the chair, both of us laughing.

Ashley comes stumbling over out of nowhere and falls onto the front of our chair looking a bit disheveled. Speaking of trouble. "There you are! Alex said to find youuuuuuu," she slurs. "He said we have to leave *right now*." She imitates Alex, pointing her finger and giggling.

"Ugh, crap." I sigh. This night went from amazing to shit in about five seconds flat. "Jeez Ash, how much did you drink?" I don't know what she could have gotten into inside; we weren't even out here for that long.

She narrows her eyes. "Hey! It's your guys' fault for being the beer-pong champion couple supreme," she shoots back, still pointing her finger at me.

Lucas laughs. "Guess she has a point there," he says,

and shrugs at me. "Alright, let's get you home." He slowly rises from behind me and tosses her over his shoulder.

"Put me down!" she squeals, laughing at him as he heads inside carrying her.

I stay put, watching them in amusement, and if I'm honest with myself, admiring his backside.

After a few feet he turns around to see me still sitting on the chair. "Coming?" he asks, grinning at me.

I nod and pull myself up to follow after them. It's not till then that I remember Jake and his sour mood and wonder what kind of shitstorm is coming.

CHAPTER 6

Monday morning comes around and I'm grabbing my books from my locker when I feel someone tug a strand of my hair. I whip around expecting to see Mark, but instead there is Lucas looking adorable in jeans and a hoodie, smiling down at me. My stomach does a flip—there are those damn butterflies again.

"Morning, beautiful," he says, tucking the strand behind my ear and leaning against his locker.

More like murder hornets.

"Hi." I smile back and try to calm my heartbeat.

"How was the rest of your weekend?"

"It was good. Just laid low after Friday. Ash kept me up late when we got home. She insisted on making pizza bagels and singing Beyoncé's greatest hits at the top of her lungs." I roll my eyes, remembering how hard it was to keep her at a normal decibel and not wake up my parents.

The corner of his mouth lifts with amusement. "Beyoncé, huh?"

"Oh yeah," I say, nodding dramatically.

He laughs and shakes his head. "Cute. Anyway, sorry the night got cut short. I was hoping to spend a little more time with you."

This thrills me, obviously, but I try to play it cool. "Oh you were, were you?" I lift an eyebrow.

He smirks back at me. "Maybe we can make that happen soon?" he asks, then quickly backs a step away from me.

I look over my shoulder to see Alex approaching us. Lucas busies himself with his locker.

"Hey, have you guys seen Jake?" Alex asks us.

I shake my head. "No, I've been trying to stay out of his way since Friday. He was in a pissy mood all weekend. Ash and I tried to make him pancakes Saturday morning and he blatantly ignored us and walked out of the kitchen."

"Interesting." Alex nods, scratching the back of his neck.

I'm not sure what my brother's problem is, but he's being a bit dramatic. Trying to stir up trouble with that Chloe remark and then walking away was such a dick move. I should be pissed at *him*. So what, Lucas and I flirted a little? Nothing even happened. I'm not a little kid anymore, and it was short-lived anyway. Right after Ash found us on the lounge chair, we met Alex inside and he drove us home. Jake was nowhere to be found when we left, and must have stayed out late because he still wasn't home when I finally wrangled Ash to bed.

The bell rings, and Lucas shuts his locker.

Alex hitches his backpack on his shoulder. "Alright, don't worry about him. I'll find him later," he says to me, and takes off down the hall.

As Lucas turns to follow him, his hand grazes mine

and our eyes catch. My breath hitches as he winks at me. "Have a good day, Li," he says softly, his eyes dancing at me.

I try to control my smile as I walk to class.

Disappointment clouds my high when I realize Lucas was about to ask me to hang out before Alex interrupted us. This is all so bizarre, I'm having trouble processing the fact that Lucas is actually into me at all. But there are actual signs here, right? Real evidence? My thoughts are a whirl in my brain as I take my seat in English. I can't help but feel giddy at the prospect of a date with Lucas. But again, my heart sinks as I remember my brother's sour expression all weekend. And how quickly Lucas stepped back from me just now when Alex showed up. Ugh, why couldn't I just have an all-consuming crush on someone else? Anyone else?

I'm chewing on my pen, lost in thought when I feel my phone vibrate with a text. I fish it out of my bag and see it's from Lucas.

You look pretty today

I almost fall out of my chair. I clamp my lips down to keep from grinning at my phone. My classmates must think I'm a crazy person. **Smooth**, I reply with a winky-face emoji. *Play it cool, Lila.* **Bet you say that to all the girls...** I add.

A minute goes by and he doesn't respond. Dread pools in my stomach. Ugh, am I going overboard playing hard to get? I don't know how to do this! I need a handbook or something. Flirting does not come naturally to me; I'm flying by the seat of my pants here. I stare daggers through my screen, willing something to happen. My heart lurches when suddenly I see the blue bubbles that indicate he's typing start, then stop, then start again. Is he also having trouble crafting the perfect flirty text?

Finally he sends: ***Sorry, teacher watching…***

Phew. I blow out a breath.

Another one comes through: ***So, you ARE jealous!***

An audible snort escapes me, and my hand immediately flies to my face as I duck down in my seat. I peek up through my eyelashes to see a few of my classmates staring at me. I duck my head lower, letting my hair fall over my face. Now they really must think I'm crazy.

Jealous? Ha, jealous! He's not even mine to be jealous about! Is he? What exactly is happening here?

While I'm debating a clever response, another text comes through: ***I'm flattered ;)***

I'm careful not to move a muscle this time as the rush of adrenaline coursing through my body threatens to lift me from my seat.

Good to know… I respond, then add a heart-eyes emoji, shocking myself at how bold I'm being. Maybe I'm not so bad at this after all. Ash would be so proud.

Later that day, I'm in the kitchen doing homework when Jake and Alex walk in after hockey practice. After raiding the fridge, they sit down across the table from me with their snacks.

"How was practice?" I ask, trying to make conversation.

My brother just grunts at me. Slight improvement—at least I'm getting some verbal feedback today.

I put my pen down and frown at him. "Okay, what is your problem? Just say it." I've had enough of his attitude.

He rolls his eyes like I'm the most annoying thing in the world. "Okay, fine. You girls were drunk and sloppy at the party and made fools of yourselves flirting with everyone. It was embarrassing."

I flinch at his words and the cutting animosity in his tone. I can only gape at him, shocked. "What? I most certainly did not!" I look at Alex for help, baffled by this accusation, which is completely false.

He looks just as puzzled as me and it takes him a minute to swallow the handful of chips in his mouth. "Dude, what are you talking about?" he asks Jake.

My brother scoffs at us both. "Last party you'll ever be going to with us," he says to me. He shakes his head and takes a bite of his sandwich.

My face grows hot with outrage. I can't believe what I'm hearing right now. I wasn't drunk at all—I barely even had a whole beer!

"You were the one who was wasted and being a total jerk." I point my finger at him. "And yes, maybe Ash got a little drunk," I concede, "but I wasn't even buzzed. So no, you couldn't be more wrong. Alex, back me up here." I turn to Alex, my eyes pleading.

Alex shifts in his chair, confusion clouding his expression. "She's right, she really wasn't drunk, bro. She beat us at beer pong and barely touched her cups at all."

But the truth falls on deaf ears.

The chair scrapes the floor as my brother stands up abruptly. "Whatever. I know what I saw. Fuck you both," he says, nostrils flaring. He tosses his plate and uneaten sandwich in the sink and storms out of the kitchen.

I let out a breath I didn't realize I was holding and look at Alex through threatening tears. "What the fuck?" My brain is still processing what the hell just happened.

He sighs and leans back in his chair, rubbing the back of his neck. "That was crazy."

I hunch forward and drop my head in my hands. "What the hell is his problem?" I grumble. I peer at Alex through my fingers. "You know I really wasn't drunk, right? Was I acting sloppy?" I ask him, now second-guessing my own memory.

He leans toward me, ducking his head to meet my gaze. "Not at all, I swear. I would have taken you home sooner. The second I saw how drunk Ash was getting, I said time to go." He hooks a thumb over his shoulder.

I let out a frustrated groan into my hands. "What a dick." Well, my brother will obviously never let me live my life. Flirting with everyone? *One person.* Not "everyone." And it was harmless. Well, kind of. Ugh, this is so not ideal. He'll never let me out again.

Alex clears his throat, and I pick my head up from my hands.

"What?" I ask.

He eyes me warily. "Well, he wasn't exactly wrong about all of it."

My chest squeezes. "What's that supposed to mean?" I narrow my eyes at him.

"You *were* flirting with *Lucas*," he states plainly, emphasizing Lucas's name.

I don't know why this surprises me. Alex is pretty smart, so I'm thinking he's obviously known about my feelings for Lucas, but he hasn't ever addressed it before.

48

I'm sure he's picked up on it over the years, especially after that day in the cafeteria when I asked about Chloe.

I feign ignorance and rear my head back. "What are you talking about?"

He lifts a brow. "Oh, come on. I'm not blind, I can read you like a book. *And* Lucas. And you both were definitely flirting *with each other*. So what's up? Is something going on between you two?"

I chew on my lip and look down, ignoring his question and avoiding his penetrating gaze. My face grows hotter by the second.

He raps his knuckles on the table. "Lila, hello?" He squints at me, waiting for a response.

I finally look up to meet his eyes. "Was it that obvious?" I manage to squeak out.

He laughs without mirth. "Um, to me, yes. And clearly to Jake. And if something *is* happening, Lucas should really man up and speak to him about it. Fuck, he should speak to me about it." His voice rises a few octaves.

I feel the agitation coming off of him and cringe back in my chair. "Okay, okay." I put my hands out to calm him. "But I really don't know what's going on. Something just shifted at the party. Things feel different now. I don't feel like this is only in my head anymore." I shrug and look back down at my hands wringing themselves in my lap.

"Lila, you've been in love with Luke since you were practically in diapers. I see the way he looks at you too, you know." My eyes shoot back up to this, I guess he did pick up on it, after all. "He's always treated you differently than other girls. Kinder, with more patience. You can tell he's comfortable being himself around you. There's clearly a connection between you guys." He

49

pauses for a beat, and I know what's coming next. "It's just that he is Jake's best friend—well, *other* best friend. *Our* best friend. And you're like our little sister. It's kind of crossing a line. And if you are going to cross that line, the right thing to do would be to talk to Jake before anything happens between you guys," he says, leaning back in his chair, his jaw set.

Sensible Alex. His reaction is totally on-brand: insightful, compassionate and morally sound. Obviously he's right, and I want to believe that Lucas and I are the kind of people who would do the right thing. I just think this has taken us both by surprise; we're still navigating new territory here. And we're both clearly terrified of Jake's reaction. Call us cowards all you want, Jake isn't going to be okay with this.

I let out an incredulous snort. "Jake will have a shit-fit." I point in the direction of the doorway he just stormed through. "There's no way he'll receive any of this well. And what was that bullshit about Chloe? He just said that to embarrass Luke and piss him off when we were having fun."

Alex sighs and rubs his eyes. "Yeah, you're probably right. And I don't know what that Chloe thing was about. Look, everyone is anxious about graduating this year. He's stressed about college, and not in the best place right now. Which is also a reason not to go sneaking around behind his back. It could totally send him off the edge. This is shit timing, Li." He gives me a sympathetic look. "Seriously though, you need to talk to Lucas. I don't want this getting ugly and ruining the rest of our senior year." He holds my gaze for a beat to make sure I'm grasping the gravity of his words.

I give him a curt nod. I know he means business.

CHAPTER 7

"Shh!" I hiss at Ashley as we creep down the stairs to the first floor of my house. I'm trying so hard to be light on my feet and not make any noise. She, on the other hand, sounds like an elephant clomping step by step. I can't remember which step is the creaky one, but I know it's here and I don't want to wake up my parents.

My house isn't very big, and the stairs are right in front of their bedroom door (which is open a sliver) so this either really brave, or really stupid, or—probably—both.

By the grace of God, we noiselessly make our way down to the first floor, pass through the kitchen and out the sliding doors into the yard.

We both exhale when the door is firmly shut behind us. "Well that was intense," she says to me, smiling.

I lean over and put my hand on my chest, steadying my heartbeat. "I seriously almost had a heart attack."

We make our way out the back gate and stop at the side of the house where I stashed a bag of clothes earlier. This is our strategy—we sneak out in pajamas and then change into our clothes outside. Then later, we change back before we sneak back in. So if we did happen to get caught, it wouldn't look so bad to my parents if they see us sneaking out in pajamas. I mean, how much trouble could we get into wearing pajamas, anyway?

We shimmy into our jeans and boots, stuff our PJs in the bag and hide it back in the bushes. Then we run up the street to where Lucas and Mark are waiting for us in Mark's car, parked a few houses away. I vaguely told Lucas that I needed to talk to him in person, not wanting to get into Jake's whole dramatic scene over text. We agreed to meet up tonight at John's, and since Alex and Jake are going out with some girls in the city, I can hopefully get around my brother's no-more-parties decree. Ash and I agreed it was a good opportunity for Lucas and me to talk without them around, but also in a group setting. Lucas texted me an hour ago offering to pick us up and warned me Mark was already wasted, so I have no idea what we're walking into right now.

We get to the car and jump in the backseat, and sure enough Mark swings around from the passenger seat where he's absolutely shitfaced and gives us a huge, drunk grin. "Liiiiiilaaaa!" he slurs, his eyes almost shut.

Ugh, I hate sloppy drunks. "Jesus, what the hell did you drink?"

"Don't get me started," Lucas says, shaking his head. "If I had to estimate, about a bottle of vodka. Then he made me the designated driver of his own car."

"Dude, chill," Mark whisper-shouts, then turns back to us. "You're both so pretty." He burps, leans out the window and pukes all over the side of the car.

"Oh my God!" Ashley and I both scream in unison and shrink back in our corners.

"What the fuck, Mark? Ash, let's go back," I yell with alarm. I absolutely hate puke.

Mark turns back to us giggling, glassy-eyed, vomit dribbling down his chin.

"Gross," Ash says, wrinkling her nose.

I look away, unable to stare straight at him, and scramble for the door handle. "No way! I cannot be in this car," I say, shuddering.

Lucas laughs at my hysterics. "Lila, relax. We'll just take him home first. It'll take five minutes." He opens both back windows. "There, fresh air will help. Hang tight." He turns up the music, and I squeeze Ash's hand, praying Mark doesn't throw up on us.

I think I hold my breath the whole five-minute drive to Mark's house. We pull into the driveway and Lucas gets out and walks around the car to where Mark is basically comatose in the passenger seat.

"Oh man, you are gonna be so pissed tomorrow when you have to clean this shit up," he says, assessing the mess on the passenger side. He carefully opens the car door so he doesn't get puke on himself and attempts to pull Mark out. "I don't suppose either of you want to lend a hand?" He peers in the back window at us, smirking at our horrified faces.

All of a sudden the front door of Mark's house flies open, and his dad comes bounding down the steps in his bathrobe and slippers. "Never a dull moment with you boys," he mutters as he takes in the current situation, and walks over to help Lucas lift Mark out of the car. He sees us huddled in the back. "Oh, hey girls, I hope you have more sense than this sloppy disaster," he says, gesturing at his son.

If I wasn't so grossed out I would laugh at the fact that he's not even mad, like this is just par for the course. Typical—guys have it so much better than girls. My parents would have an absolute heart attack. In fact, the reason we had to sneak out in the first place is my ridiculously strict 11 p.m. curfew.

It takes them a good five minutes to haul Mark's ass out of the car, up the front steps and into the house.

Once they're out of earshot, I look over at Ash. "What if this is a sign? This was a bad idea," I say, my voice laced with fear.

She raises an eyebrow. "Yeah, a sign to lay off the vodka. Would you calm down? The puke has you all crazy. What are you worried about?"

"Oh, ya know, just that Jake and Alex will find out we snuck out with Lucas and kill us? Or my parents will wake up and see that we're gone and kill us? Or Jake will tell my parents and they'll all kill us?" My face flushes, and I'm bordering on hysterical now.

She snorts. "Lila, nobody is killing anyone. That's why we're going to the party, so if Jake does find out, you two won't be alone. You'll be in a social setting."

"I don't think that'll matter," I reply, visions of doom still dancing in my brain.

She turns to face me. "You can't let Jake dictate your life. The plan was for you and Lucas to discuss how to move forward. You need to actually talk to do that."

I lift a shoulder. "I guess we could've just had a phone call?" My voice rises an octave at the end.

The door to the house opens, and I shush her.

"It's too late now. Just stick with the plan. We'll be fine," she whispers, shushing me back.

Lucas opens Ash's door and hooks a thumb over his shoulder. "Mark's dad is going to drop us off at John's so we don't have to drive around in this puke bucket. Come on, hop out." He gestures to the other car in Mark's driveway.

I grimace as Ash shrugs and steps out of the car.

Lucas leans in for my hand to help me out. "I'm sorry about this," he whispers to me with an apologetic smile.

I can't help but smile back and tell him it's fine.

But it's not fine. This is so weird and embarrassing—I wonder if Mark's dad recognizes me as Jake's little sister. He has definitely seen me over the years at their hockey games.

After tucking us in the back, Lucas gets in the passenger seat up front. We listen silently as they chat about hockey and Lucas potentially playing next year in college. Lucas easily volleys back the small talk, and thankfully there's little attention on us in the back. I finally relax as we pull onto John's street with no comments about who I am and why we're with Lucas without Jake.

When we arrive, Ash bounds into the house while I hang back waiting for Lucas, who's promising Mark's dad he won't drink and drive. Once he finally leaves, Lucas walks over and grabs my hand and leads me inside. As usual, I feel butterflies whenever he touches me. A stupid little gesture like this from him and I'm a goner, no matter what the situation.

Inside, we say our hellos and head into the kitchen to grab drinks.

Lucas opens the fridge and hands me a beer, then

takes one for himself. He eyes me warily. "Are you okay? You look a little green. Where did Ashley go?" he asks, looking around for her.

"Not sure." I eye the crowd over his shoulder, hoping I can keep a very low profile at this party. "And yes, I'm fine," I add as a shudder racks my body, my mind replaying the scene in the car. I shake my head, trying to erase the image seared into my brain.

"Ah, that's right. I forgot about your vomit phobia," he says, nodding his head in understanding. "That must have really freaked you out. I'm glad you resisted the urge to flee," he says and walks over to me and tugs a lock of my hair.

I smile and look up at him through my lashes, oddly moved that he remembered my weird little quirk. "I'm glad, too."

He tucks the lock of hair behind my ear, continuing to gaze into my eyes.

My heart starts to pound. I hope he doesn't hear it, or see it pulsing out of my chest. On the one hand, I've been waiting for this forever. On the other, am I ready for it? What's going to happen? Does he actually, really like me? How far will this go? He's leaving for college soon. Not to mention Alex's voice in my head not to go behind Jake's back. Or the fact that my brother will probably murder me if he finds out I'm here right now. A million thoughts swirl through my brain at once, leaving me reeling. I hope Lucas doesn't see any of this playing out on my face, but he seems to sense my inner turmoil.

He tilts my chin up with a finger, studying my face. "Hey, where's your head at right now?" he asks softly.

"Right here?" my voice warbles, and it comes out sounding like a question.

He eyes me critically. "Come with me." He grabs my hand, leading me deeper into the kitchen into a small alcove that's actually a pantry.

I pretend to be preoccupied looking at the contents of the shelves.

He looks at me with concern. "What's wrong, Lila?"

"Nothing. Nothing at all. I'm fine…" I reply, shaking my head.

The look on his face says he's not buying it. "But…?" he prompts.

I sigh. "But I just think maybe we should talk to Jake before anything happens. Is anything going to happen? What's actually happening here?" I grimace and clamp my mouth shut to keep from blabbing, aware of how pathetic I sound.

The corner of his mouth lifts with amusement. "Do you want something to happen?" he asks, quirking an eyebrow at me.

I feel my face light on fire and throw my hands up to cover it in embarrassment.

A laugh escapes his lips. "I'm just teasing you." He reaches out and pulls my hands away so he can look into my eyes. "Of course something is happening," he says with a grin. "And I know I should talk to Jake. I guess I'm just trying to enjoy these moments I get with you before all hell breaks loose. You know how your brother can be." He sighs and scrubs a hand over his jaw.

"I know, but that's exactly why Alex said we should tell him first," I blurt out without thinking.

He freezes and his eyes go wide. "Wait, you talked to *Alex* about this?" He takes a step back, his hand grabbing the back of his neck. "That's just great, Lila. He's even worse than Jake."

"No, I didn't tell him anything," I exclaim, taking a step toward him, wringing my hands. "Well, not really. I mean, he kind of figured it out, Lucas. He's not blind. Even you said we were flirting the other night." I look at him pointedly. "And Jake totally blew up at me the other day in front of Alex, claiming I was wasted at the party and embarrassed him by flirting with everyone."

His jaw drops at my words. "*What?* That's crazy! You were not! Jesus, what a shitshow." He leans against the shelves and sighs, closing his eyes and resting his head back.

Crap, he looks miserable. What do I do now? I try to think of something to say, but come up short.

After a few moments of heavy silence, he gestures at me. "Come here." He reaches out to grab my hand and pulls me toward him.

I release the breath I didn't even realize I'd been holding and close the gap between us.

He reaches his arms around my body. "I'm sorry. This all just kind of caught me by surprise." He squeezes me against his chest and rests his chin on the top of my head. "I know the stakes are high here since you're Jake's little sister, but I can't help how I feel. I'm crazy about you, Lila."

My stomach does a somersault. Did he really just say that? I peel my head back from his chest and look up into his eyes, trying to seek the truth in them. "Really?" I ask.

"Yes, really," he answers with emphasis and sincerity. He holds my gaze, and a rush of heat shoots through my body. His eyes trail down to my lips and my breath hitches in my throat. I wonder if this is the moment Lucas will actually kiss me.

I don't have to wonder for long, because then he does.

He bends forward and brushes his lips against mine. Lightly at first, so subtle I'm not even sure it happened. He pulls back an inch, studying my face.

I reach up with my hands and pull him back down to me. This time the kiss isn't subtle at all. It's intense and passionate and full of everything I've been holding in for sixteen years. I get lost in this kiss—I feel dizzy, intoxicated, like I never want it to end.

He moans and slowly pulls away, his hands firmly on my waist, holding me in place.

"Wow," I whisper, at the risk of sounding my age.

"Told you I was crazy about you," he says with a faint smile on his lips. He tugs me in closer and I go willingly, wrapping my arms around his waist and breathing him in. He smells so good, like soap, with a hint of a woodsy cologne and men's deodorant. I wish I could bottle it up.

"What are we gonna do, Lucas?" I groan.

"I'll talk to Jake," he promises.

I look up into his eyes, and he repeats it wholeheartedly. "I don't want to come between you two," I tell him. "The last thing I want is to ruin your senior year."

"Let me handle it," he says. "I promise it'll be okay."

"If you say so," I say skeptically. "Maybe we should go find Ash, we've been in here for a while."

He nods and gives my waist one last squeeze, then takes my hand and leads me back out the way we came in.

Alex walks into the kitchen at the exact moment we exit the pantry. I stop short, stuck like a deer in headlights. He does a double-take at my face, then his eyes dart to Lucas's hand holding mine and his expression immediately darkens. He looks back up to me with anger in his eyes. "Lila? I didn't know you were gonna be here."

My heart throbs in my ears. He is pissed. I knew coming here without telling him was a bad idea. I have no idea what to say right now; I have no excuse for my deception but my own cowardice.

"Alex...hi," I stammer, and drop Lucas's hand.

Lucas senses my discomfort and steps in. "It was a last-minute thing," he says. "I picked them up on my way over." A valiant attempt to save me that falls flat.

Alex raises his eyebrows at me, ignoring Lucas completely. "Considering the hour, I'd say you snuck out?"

Busted. He knows my curfew, and it's well past that right now.

I wince and look down at the floor, my face burning with shame.

"You obviously completely ignored what I said the other day." His tone is sharper now.

My eyes shoot to his, pleading with him to take it down a notch.

No luck. "Now you're sneaking out in the middle of the night, and behind my back?" Okay, he's furious. He finally looks over at Lucas. "And what the hell are you thinking, man?" He shakes his head and closes his eyes. "Jake is going to fucking kill you," he breathes out.

"Jake is going to kill who?" my brother asks as he rounds the corner and stops short when he sees us, shock freezing his face. "*Lila?* Hell no. What the fuck are you doing here?" His eyes narrow as he registers Lucas next to me. "Luke, did you bring her here?" His voice rises five octaves.

This is bad. Real bad. You can cut the tension in this kitchen with a knife. I can actually feel my own anxiety pouring off my body in waves. I'm praying this scene stays contained to the kitchen and nobody else in the house is hearing this right now, but it doesn't seem like I'll be so lucky. People start popping their heads in, wondering what the commotion is all about.

My panic level skyrockets at the influx of witnesses. I catch Alex's eye, silently pleading with him to somehow help me out here, but the hard set of his jaw suggests that will not be happening. There's disappointment written all over his face. I'm on my own. My brother's hostile glare burns a hole through my forehead, and I shrink back, knocking into Lucas's front.

Lucas's hands find my shoulders and his grip tightens, steadying me. "I was going to talk to you, Jake." I'm in awe of how steady his voice sounds. "I just didn't get the chance yet..." He trails off.

I don't dare speak; I probably couldn't get a word out anyway. My insides feel wobbly, like I might puke myself right now.

"Talk to me about what? You think I'll give you permission to fuck my little sister? Dude, you're my best friend. What the hell are you thinking?" My brother spits his words out sharply, his eyes blazing with fury.

"No, it's not like that, man. I'd never disrespect her like that!" Lucas's voice is rising now too. This is so embarrassing. At this point, basically the entire senior class is crammed into the kitchen watching this go down. My life is imploding in front of everyone like immersive theater. Have I mentioned I hate being the center of attention? I can feel my face turn from red to crimson.

Ashley finally makes an appearance, pushing her way through the crowd.

"Where the hell have you been?" I hiss at her when she reaches my side—finally able to find my voice.

"Sorry, sorry!" she whispers, and looks between the guys who are locked in a wordless brawl of murderous glares. "Alright guys, why don't we go outside? No more to see here people, keep it moving," she says to everyone as she opens the kitchen door and ushers us all outside.

I'm kind of shocked anyone actually listens to her, but people seem to be bored of the show and start to disperse out of the kitchen as we make our way to the mercifully empty backyard. Jake walks to the end of the patio with his hands in his hair. Lucas leans against the house, face pinched with contrition, staring at the ground. Ashley has her back against the door so nobody else can come out to witness this fiasco.

"I told you this was going to happen," Alex mutters to me under his breath.

"Well I guess you were right, okay? I'm sorry! Now can you just help me please so they don't kill each other?" I hiss back at him.

"What do you want me to do about it?" he spits back, giving me a patent glare, which I volley right back.

"I don't know. Something! Anything?" He just stares at me wordlessly. "Ugh fine, thanks for nothing," I say as I walk over to Jake.

Guess I'll have to take a shot at defusing the situation myself.

"Look Jake, we aren't sneaking around behind your back. It just happened. This is the first time we're even hanging out without you. I'm sorry you feel ambushed," I say, trying to lace my words with as much remorse as possible.

The rigid set of his shoulders and tense line of his jaw tell me he isn't buying it. I can feel the anger vibrating from his body.

Lucas attempts to back me up, still keeping his distance from across the patio. "Yeah, Jake, this is a very new development. And I swear I was going to talk to you about it. I genuinely have feelings for her. You have to believe me. I'd never do anything to jeopardize our friendship."

Jake silences him with a sideways look. He closes the distance between them in three large steps. I back up out of his way. He reaches out and pokes a finger into Lucas's chest. "But you just did," he states with emphasis. Then he turns around and stalks out of the yard without another word.

"Well, shit." Ashley blows out a long breath that I'm positive all of us have been holding. Alex gapes at her, incredulous. "What? You guys weren't even supposed to be here," she exclaims.

He flings his arms open. "Are you serious right now? What did you think, we wouldn't find out that you were here? All of our friends are in there!" His nostrils flare as he points at the house. "Was anyone using their heads tonight? You girls need to go home. Now. Come on, I'll drive you. And as for you"—he pauses to glare at Lucas, who looks hunched over himself at this point—"you better fix this. I'm not having our senior year ruined because of your poor fucking judgment." And with that, he gestures for Ash and me to start moving.

As I follow Alex to the car, I look back over my shoulder at Lucas, who's bent over with his head hanging in his hands. It's the saddest thing I've ever seen, and I wish there was something I could do to comfort him, but I'm powerless as Alex drags me away.

CHAPTER 8

It's been a rough two days since the disastrous party. Jake won't even look at me. Alex is also icing me out, and I haven't heard a word from Lucas. I sent him multiple apology texts but got no response all weekend. Let's just say I've been glued to my phone, trying my best to will it to ring, but no such luck.

After Alex dropped us off Friday night and we snuck back into my house, it took Ash a good hour to talk me off the ledge. All I could see was Jake's face twisted in fury. I felt terrible. I couldn't wrap my head around the fact that the whole disaster actually went down in real life and wasn't just a bad movie I'd wasted my night on. *And* in front of half the school, no less. I barely slept a wink the whole night. I kept waiting for Jake to come home and out me to my parents for sneaking out, but he never did. I might have preferred that to the hardcore silent treatment he and Alex are doling out instead.

When he finally came home Sunday night, I tried to corner him, begging him to at least look at me, but he wasn't having it. I've never felt so guilty in my life. The last thing I want is to ruin his and Lucas' friendship. And the second-to-last thing is losing any shot I had with Lucas. I don't know what I thought was going to happen; going to the party seems like such an obviously bad idea in hindsight. So, I've been wallowing in my room by myself for the past few days. Ash keeps trying to pry me out, but I just can't summon the energy. My emotions have been running the gamut from shame to panic to hopelessness and back to humiliation. I'm so emotionally exhausted I can barely lift my head from my pillow on Monday morning.

At school I keep my head down, feeling all eyes on me as I walk down the hallway with a knot in my stomach. Who knows how many of my fellow classmates saw our theatrical debut in John's kitchen. I know I'm probably being irrational; it's unlikely anyone even cares that much about my drama. People are too caught up in their own lives. But still, I can't shake this deep feeling of vulnerability and embarrassment.

I'm doing my best to hide behind my locker when Ashley appears and pulls me into a hug. I lean into her, trying to hold back the tears threatening to spill from my eyes. You'd think the well would dry up after a whole weekend of waterworks.

She gives me a sympathetic squeeze. "It's gonna be okay. Any word from the guys yet?" she asks softly.

I hang my head in shame. "No, crickets. Jake stayed at Alex's all weekend and won't even look in my direction. Alex is still pissed too. And Lucas won't answer any of my texts." I try to keep my voice low and look around, making sure nobody is paying attention to us before I continue. "I feel like everyone is staring at me. Ash, what am I supposed to do? I knew this was too good to be true," I cry, leaning my head back against the locker.

She grabs my shoulders and spins me to face her. "Look at me, Lila." She's using her no-nonsense voice, eyes boring into mine. "These boys love you. You are smart, beautiful, kind, amazing—how can anyone be blamed for liking you? Deep down, Jake and Alex know this. They *will* forgive you. And as for Lucas, he's not mad at *you*. He's probably mad at himself for how it went down. I'm sure he's kicking himself for not having a conversation with Jake first."

I know she's probably right, and I love her for trying to make me feel better, but I'm having trouble seeing reason right now. I close my eyes and let out a long breath. When I open them she's still staring at me, her face now softened with compassion.

"This will blow over," she says with an emphatic head nod.

"I think I'm just gonna go home," I say, defeated, as I grab my books and shut my locker. "I just can't be here today." I feel shaky and nauseous and can only think about living this day curled up, engulfed by the blankets on my bed.

Ash nods and puts her arm around me for one last side-hug. "I'll stop by on my way home to check on you later," she promises.

I'm walking out of school and through the parking lot, looking forward to the walk home to clear my head, when I see Lucas getting out of his car. He sees me and instantly freezes. According to his face and the hard set of his jaw, I'm the last person he wants to run into right now.

But I don't care; I need to talk to him. I ignore my churning stomach and head in his direction.

His eyes sweep the parking lot to make sure we're alone, which just stokes the fire of humiliation already roaring inside me.

I stop a few feet from him. "Hi," I say softly.

"Hi," he replies, looking everywhere but in my eyes.

I try to speak through the lump in my throat. "I am so, so sorry, Lucas. I feel terrible." I wring my hands and will him to look at my face.

He sighs and scrubs a hand down his chin, staring at his feet. "It's not your fault, Lila. It's my fault. I should've talked to Jake before I let anything happen between us. This is on me, I messed up here." His tone is laced with remorse.

I inch toward him, trying harder to make eye contact. "What can I do? How can I help make this better?"

He finally lifts his eyes to mine and I see an ocean of sadness mixed with regret. In that instant I know what's coming next, and I'm powerless to stop it. "Look, Lila, I meant every word I said in that pantry. I am crazy about you. And I really wish things were different, but Jake and Alex aren't just my best friends, they're my brothers. They're the closest thing I have to family, besides my mom. I can't jeopardize that any more than I have already. I just can't. I'm really sorry, but this was a mistake. It can't go any further." He shakes his head, shoulders slumped in defeat.

I take a step back and my hands fly to my stomach, feeling his words like a punch to my gut. I'm speechless. I couldn't even argue if I wanted to. The pained expression on his face is the last thing I see before he turns and walks away from me, leaving me standing alone in the parking lot. I don't know what I was expecting, but after the other night, after finally admitting our feelings out in the open, I didn't think he would just take them back. I understand where he's coming from, but I'm still beyond crushed.

I walk home on autopilot with tears streaming down my face. I don't even realize I made it the whole way until I notice Jake's car in the driveway. He must have come home early too since he was gone already when I left for school.

I wipe my face and give myself a pep talk as I walk into the house. Alex and Jake are sitting on the couch in the living room, locked in a serious conversation. They stop talking and look up as they see me walk in. They both look beyond exhausted. Jake avoids my eyes, but I steel my resolve and walk farther into the room until I'm standing in front of them. I'm determined to hash this out.

"I'm really sorry for what happened." I start to choke up, but power through. "We never wanted to go behind your back or keep it from you. It just happened, and I know that's not an excuse, and you have every right to be mad. But it's over between us now, I swear. Your friendship means more to him than anything." I let out a shaky breath and sit on the arm of the couch across from them.

Jake grunts and rolls his eyes. Alex's expression softens as he hears the pain in my voice and he gets up to comfort me, but I hold my arm out to stop him.

I lock eyes with him. "You both have to believe me. Nothing is more important, to *either* of us, than you two." My voice breaks on the last word, and he closes the gap between us and pulls me in for a hug. I collapse with a sob against his chest.

"It'll be okay, Lila," he whispers while rubbing my back.

"So that's it?" Jake exclaims and stands up. "You just expect me to act like nothing happened and move on like my best friend didn't betray me?"

I pull away from Alex to address my brother. "Nothing did happen, Jake. It was one night! *One party!* In over ten years of friendship. You're just going to throw that friendship away? Lucas feels terrible. Please just talk to him," I beg, trying to suppress another sob from escaping.

Alex shrugs a shoulder and looks at my brother. "She has a point, Jake. We've been friends for a long time. He's been calling us both for days now, trying to apologize. I think we should at least hear him out. They obviously both regret it."

Jake unclenches his hands and lets out a slow breath, considering Alex's words. I know he's hurt and feels betrayed right now, but he has to know how much Lucas loves him and values their friendship. I'm praying he remembers that and can find a way to forgive him. He's silent for a moment as he contemplates this in his head. "Fine, I'll hear him out," he concedes after a beat. He narrows his eyes, assessing me critically. "Are you sure it's over?"

I nod and reach up to wipe my eyes, powerless against the new tears escaping. "Yes, I'm sure. It didn't even start." I breathe out this last part and look away.

He grabs his phone and keys off the table before walking to the door. "Come on Al, let's go." He gestures for Alex to follow.

Alex hesitates and looks over at me. "Are you sure you're okay?"

I nod and meet his gaze. "Yes, I'm okay. Go. Please, Alex, just let Lucas try to fix this."

He nods and offers me a small smile, then turns to follow Jake out the door.

I sit back, letting the tears flow freely, and hope my brother has the ability to forgive his best friend.

CHAPTER 9

SUMMER 2016

"Who wants another beer?" Alex asks as he heads inside to grab another round. Ashley, Jake and I all raise our hands. We're sitting in my backyard around the firepit, debating our next move for the night. It's the Thursday before July Fourth weekend and we decided to take advantage of the empty house and BBQ since my parents are away for the holiday.

Alex hands out the beers and I sit back in my chair and kick my feet up on the table. I can barely move, I'm so full; we just stuffed ourselves with cheeseburgers and chicken wings. But I'm also filled with a warm contentment humming through my body. It's my first summer back home after college, and I forgot how much I missed my people.

Alex sits down next to me and his phone chirps with a text. He reads it out loud—some of their old teammates are going to Catch, one of the bars that we used to hang out at in high school that was suspiciously lenient on fake IDs.

"That place is still standing?" Jake asks, looking surprised. "People still go there?"

Alex laughs and confirms with a nod. "Yeah, sounds like it will be a mini high school reunion. Should be fun. Will be great to see all the guys. What do you think?" He looks around at all of us.

I inwardly wince as my happy mood gets crushed. I look at Ash, who reads my mind as soon as our eyes meet. Which guys? Will *he* be there?

She cocks her head sympathetically as I watch her listen to my inner chatter.

I need a way to abort this plan. "Why don't we just hang here? Nobody feels like driving anyway." I shrug, making a futile attempt to sway the group.

Ash shifts her eyes away with a faint smile on her lips. She knows exactly what I'm doing, but she stays quiet in solidarity.

"I can drive. I've only had one beer so far," Jake offers, placing the fresh one Alex just handed him down on the table. "I was planning on taking it easy tonight anyway."

Anxiety builds in my chest as I realize my chances of getting out of this are shrinking by the second.

"Let me just go in and change my shirt." Jake frowns as he inspects the ketchup stain on the front of his polo.

"I'm gonna fix my makeup real quick," Ash says as she stands and follows him inside, giving my shoulder a sympathetic squeeze as she passes.

Fuck. I rack my brain for an excuse. I stay in my seat, chewing my lip.

Alex throws the empty beers in the garbage and takes the seat across from me, leaning forward with his elbows on his knees. "You're scared to see Lucas, aren't you?" he asks me.

I avoid his gaze and busy myself swiping at imaginary crumbs on the table. He can read me like a book.

"It's been over six years, Lila," he says softly.

"It's not him." I shake my head.

His face tells me he's not buying it. "Come on, it'll be fun."

I offer an eye roll. "You guys go. I'll just stay here. I can finish cleaning up..." I trail off as I look around at the impeccably tidy patio.

He catches this and smirks at me.

I lean back in my seat and sigh. I won't be getting out of this.

Alex is right: It's been over six years since Lucas walked away from me in that parking lot, leaving me feeling like the world bottomed out beneath my feet. Needless to say, we did not keep in touch. Jake wound up forgiving him—thanks to Alex's persuasion, I'm sure—but after what happened, things were tense for a long time. Between the guys, and between my brother and me. Alex forgave me immediately—unsurprising, being the compassionate person he is. They carried on with their senior year, but I didn't see much of Lucas after that day. He did his best to steer clear of me at school, and they stopped coming over to our house as much, choosing to hang at Alex's or someone else's place instead. Alex tried to assure me that they weren't purposely avoiding me, but I knew better. Whether Alex wanted to admit it to my face or not, I knew they were trying to keep Lucas and me separate. It hurt like hell being divided from my boys, but I knew I'd made my own bed, and I was just grateful that my brother forgave Lucas.

But it still didn't hurt any less.

I was pretty traumatized from the whole fiasco. After

the boys graduated and left town, I tried my hardest to focus on school and getting into college. I threw myself into academics and barely had any social life, preferring to keep my weekends low-key—staying in and watching movies with Ash or hanging out with some of our other friends from school. Ash tried to get me to date other guys, but I just didn't see the point. I knew I wouldn't get over Lucas any time soon, and I wasn't interested in any distractions. I was so focused on graduating and getting into Georgetown, on leaving this town and my memories of Lucas in the rearview as soon as possible. So I buckled down, put my head in my books and swore off guys for the rest of high school. I did not want to get attached to someone else and suffer another broken heart before I even got to college.

Once I did get to college, I started to loosen up a bit. I welcomed the anonymity of nobody knowing my business. We grew up in such a small town where everyone knows everything about one another, so I welcomed the new experience of being a little fish in a big pond. I could reinvent myself. I didn't have to be the brokenhearted little sister anymore. I made new friends, I went to parties, I joined the swim team. I even met someone that I thought would take the sting away.

Jamie and I met sophomore year on the first day of my communications class. He was cute in a nerdy way, which surprised me since he had a t-shirt with fraternity letters on it. He had floppy blond hair, big puppy dog eyes and glasses. He sat down next to me and asked me for a pen. His smile never faltered, even after he saw my eyes track down to some pens in the open bookbag at his feet. I laughed and handed him the one I was holding. After that day we became friends, studying together and occasionally hanging with his frat brothers. Our friend groups eventually intertwined, and we began spending more and more time together.

Then months later, one night at a party, we both got drunk and hooked up. Our connection was definitely not all-consuming fireworks, but we settled into an effortless companionship, which was a welcome relief after the intensity of my feelings for Lucas. We had the same taste in TV and movies, he came to cheer me on at all my swim meets, and one summer I even went home with him to Rhode Island for a few weeks.

He was easy to be around and we had a blast together, but I couldn't shake the feeling that something was missing. I tried my hardest to squash the fierce pull I felt for Lucas, this deep-rooted affection I felt in the very core of my being. I loved hanging out with Jamie, but I didn't think I was *in love* with him—it felt more like a friendship than a hot-and-heavy love affair. However, I told myself I was more than okay with it. I'd put up a wall around my heart after what happened with Lucas and was scared to death of getting hurt again. But it felt easy and safe knowing the risk of heartbreak was low. I just wasn't ready to open myself up to someone else again.

Senior year, Jamie lined up a full-time job at his dad's accounting firm back home in Rhode Island. His plan was always to follow in the family business and mine was to work in publishing back in NYC, so we decided to take some time apart to figure out the next steps in our lives. While I knew I would miss him, I also knew he wasn't the great love of my life and that our separation was inevitable. I think he felt it too; he didn't ask me to move home with him and pretty easily accepted the fact that we were headed in different directions. And anyway, I believed if we were really meant to be together, then we'd find our way back to each other.

It took a while for Jake and me to repair our relationship after what happened with Lucas. It was especially hard when he left for school, putting even more distance between us. The first year he was away, we barely spoke at all. After a while we worked our way up to a text here and there, then a phone call every couple of weeks, and finally got to a point where we started to become friends. He even visited me a few times in DC after he graduated. I want to attribute this to both of us growing up and gaining emotional maturity, but I have a feeling Alex had a lot to do with it. I'm sure he chipped away at the polar ice cap of my brother's heart and finally convinced him of the importance of family.

One night, walking home from the bar during one of Jake's visits, I mustered up enough liquid courage to broach the subject of what happened with Lucas. To my surprise, we wound up having a very mature and civilized conversation about it. He said looking back on it, he'd probably overreacted, but he felt betrayed by us and conflicted by his instinct to protect me. He didn't like the idea of any older guy taking advantage of me, and even though he knew Lucas wasn't a dirtbag, he was still a high school teenager and he didn't trust him with his little sister. He admitted to feeling bad for how he'd alienated me from his life—he just didn't know how else to deal with it. Being the emotionally stunted eighteen-year-old he was, he chose avoidance, which he wasn't proud of.

I told him I understood, we all had a lot of growing up to do. He also told me that Alex helped him to realize his and Lucas's friendship was too important to just throw away, and besides, nobody could be blamed for falling for me. I laughed at this, picturing Alex arguing that point. He laughed too, but then said Alex was right, and he really did feel bad about taking so long to close the rift between us.

I was floored by this new, openly vulnerable Jake—he'd come a long way from the angsty high schooler who left for college without a second glance. I admired his ability to be open and honest with me about his feelings, and was thrilled to move into this new stage of our relationship. After that visit I felt a deep sense of relief, like I'd been holding in a breath for the last four years and didn't even know it. Since then he's been a big part of my life, and I'm excited to be living closer to him again.

After college, Jake and Alex got an apartment together in the city, having both scored jobs at banking firms downtown. Ashley also moved back home with her family after graduation. She chose to take it easy this summer and got a job as a camp counselor, giving herself some time to figure out if she wants to apply to law school. Thanks to my communications professor, I was able to snag a summer internship at a publishing company, hoping to get my foot in the door and help me figure out what I wanted to do with my life.

I have no idea what Lucas has been up to. I'm not even sure if he's back in town. While I heard bits and pieces about him from the guys through the years, I didn't ask about him, and they didn't offer any information. That's not to say he didn't ever cross my mind. Sometimes I've found myself thinking about him while engaged in mindless tasks, like folding laundry or blow-drying my hair. I almost always thought of him while I was being intimate with Jamie, which wasn't that far a stretch since he was the only other boy I'd actually had real feelings for. But I tried to divert my mind from thoughts of him. I told myself it was silly first love, and blamed my intense emotions on crazy teenage hormones. I knew it was too good to be true from the start. I was a fool for believing him when he said he was crazy about me. If that was really true, could he just cut me out of his life without any contact for so many years? Not likely.

It doesn't matter now, it may as well have been a lifetime ago. We're all grown up and don't even know each other anymore.

Forty-five minutes—and every possible reason for me to procrastinate—later, Jake finds a parking spot right in front of the bar and we hop out of the car. I let the others go in ahead of me, while I take a deep breath and give myself one last pep talk before walking through the door.

Of course he's the first thing I see once my eyes adjust to the hazy light.

He's leaning against the bar and looks up as we walk in. My body freezes as his eyes lock on mine. For a split-second the whole world fades away and I'm transported six years back in time.

Fuck, I'm in trouble.

I'm shaken from my momentary paralysis when Ashley yanks my arm, asking me what I want to drink. I mumble something incoherent and she knowingly rolls her eyes and asks the bartender for two of whatever she already ordered for herself.

My gaze finds its way back to Lucas, who's now hugging Alex and Jake in that half hug, half slap-on the-back routine guys do. He looks good, really good; age has served him well. His brown hair has grown out some from his signature buzz cut, but is still short, cropped close to his head. And he's sporting some seriously sexy scruff on his face which somehow accentuates his chiseled jaw even more. He's kept in shape over the years; I can tell by the way his white t-shirt hugs his muscular frame. I squeeze my eyes shut and tell myself to get a grip and stop ogling his body. Maybe now that I'm a grownup I can get my shit together and not act like a tween at a Justin Bieber concert around this guy.

Ashley hands me my drink, and I gulp half of it down without even looking at it. I practically spit the beer back up as the last sip goes down the wrong pipe. My eyes water profusely and I'm bent over, sputtering, trying to catch my breath when I feel her hip check mine. My eyes lift just in time to see Lucas standing in front of us, an amused smile on his lips. I wipe the beer from my face and try to pull myself together.

Fortunately, he gives me a minute to recover gracefully and gives Ash a hug and kiss on the cheek first. He hesitates before embracing me, opting instead for a subdued verbal greeting. "Hey, Lila," he says, sizing up my reaction.

I give him an awkward smile. "Hey, Lucas." I lean in to kiss his cheek, then pull back quickly. "Good to see you." I inwardly wince and offer another small smile to disguise my insincerity before hightailing it straight to the bathroom.

Once I'm safely inside the bathroom, I lean against the door and try to slow the hammering of my heart. *Jesus Christ, Lila. Pull it together, will you?* I curse my body for reacting that way, even after six fucking years.

I'm startled by a knock on the door. "Lila, it's me. Let

me in." It's Ash. I let her in and quickly lock the door behind her, reclaiming my spot against it.

"Well that went well," she says with a glint in her eye.

"I told you I didn't want to come!" I hiss at her.

Her face splits into a grin and I'm about to ask her what the hell is so funny when I realize she's distracted by something above my head. She points to a spot on the door. "Lila + Ash = BFFL," she reads out loud, her finger trailing over the faded marker on the door.

I turn around to see it and smile as I momentarily forget my current drama and remember the night when we drunkenly defaced this tiny bathroom. It seems like a million years ago. I sigh. "If only I could travel back in time and erase him from my history," I say, leaning back against the door.

She looks back to me, sympathy softening her face. "Not possible." She squeezes my hand. "You okay?"

I cover my face with my hands and a groan escapes my throat. "I haven't seen him in over six years, and he approaches me at the exact moment beer comes out of my nose." I hang my head in humiliation.

A laugh escapes her lips and she flings a hand to her mouth. "I'm sorry, I'm sorry. But, like, only you." Her eyes dance with amusement as she shakes her head at me.

I can't help but laugh also. "Oh, man." I lean in to look at myself over the tiny mirror above the sink and wipe away the smudged mascara on my face. I take a breath and blow it out. "Okay, okay. I'm okay," I say to myself in the mirror, then turn to gesture at her to open the door.

"You got this," she says before dutifully obliging, and leads us back out to the bar.

After chatting with some old friends for a while, I

head to the bar to grab Ash and myself another round. I'm attempting to get the bartender's attention when I feel Lucas standing next to me. My stomach drops to my feet.

"You look good," he says, eyeing me guardedly.

"Thanks, you too," I reply, and pull my eyes away from his. I try to keep my tone light and my face wiped of emotion.

The moment stretches. Jesus, this is awkward. I try to Jedi mind-trick the bartender to notice me and come over to take my order already. It doesn't work.

Lucas tries again. "So how are you? How have you been?"

"Good, good. I'm fine," I say quickly, looking anywhere but at him, hoping he'll get bored of my attempt to thwart this convo and give up.

No such luck.

"Hey, look at me." He gently touches my shoulder. I don't give in. "Lila," he says with more urgency this time.

I relent with a sigh and turn to face him. His green eyes are sad, and I watch as emotion washes across his face.

He looks like he's about to apologize and I don't want to go down that road. I can't.

I pre-emptively blurt out, "How's your life, Lucas?"

He seems to understand what I'm doing. "Good. I'm good, too." He nods his head and rubs his jaw. Great, we're both good. Now that that's established, maybe we can go on avoiding each other.

I try to pull my attention away, but my eyes have a mind of their own. I follow his hands as they track down his face and over his scruff. I forgot how sexy he is up close. He's still the same Lucas, but older, more grown up. His chiseled jaw is even more pronounced, with lines that

81

could cut glass, and his skin has an early summer tan already. He shifts his weight under my gaze, and my cheeks flush as I realize I'm ogling him.

Finally, the bartender chooses now to come over and take my order. When he hands me my beers, Lucas insists on paying in spite of my vigorous objections.

After a chaste thank you, I eye my friends and make my escape. "Well, good to see you. Thanks again." I lift my beer to him and turn to go. I walk over to where Ash is watching Alex and Jake playing pool and realize he has followed me. By the expression on his face, I can tell he wants to say more, but I don't give him the chance. He's had plenty of time to reach out, to say anything he wanted to say. But no calls, no texts, no emails, not even a Facebook message.

I stand by Ash and turn my shoulder to shut him out. By Ash's empathetic look over my head, I can tell he must have a pained expression, but I don't care. I can't go down memory lane tonight. Dredging up the past isn't in the cards. It's exactly why I didn't want to come here.

He takes the hint and joins the guys on the other side of the table.

Another beer and a game of pool later, "Don't Stop Believin'" comes on the jukebox. Of course everyone goes wild and starts singing, because, well, that's just what we do when this song comes on. Ash gets up on the edge of the table, belting out the words into her microphone-beer bottle.

I sway to the music, singing along, and feel myself start to loosen up a little. Polishing off my third beer, I'm feeling warm and happy, the bar and the music bringing back memories of high school. I'm lost in a joyful nostalgia and momentarily forget about keeping tabs on Lucas.

He's been keeping his distance, but I've been hyper-aware of his location at all times. I feel like we're orbiting around each other, not getting too close for fear of spontaneous combustion. When I realize I haven't seen him for a bit and start to wonder if maybe he left, he appears next to my elbow, holding out a fresh beer.

"Peace offering?" He eyes me, an apprehensive smile playing on his lips.

I accept the beer with an amused snort. I'm too buzzed to keep up this charade any longer. He visibly relaxes at my acquiescence and cheerses me with a beer of his own. He gives me a genuine smile now, a signature Lucas smile—one that reaches his eyes, crinkling the corners, and I can't help but melt a little more. Leave it to this guy to make crow's feet irresistible.

After that, the awkward tension between us seems to evaporate. We start chatting about our lives; he asks about college, and I tell him about my internship. He tells me about work and how he's the foreman for a construction crew on a big commercial development project downtown. More old-school songs are sung, and before I know it it's 1 a.m. and I'm feeling sleepy.

He sees me yawn and checks his watch. "Damn, it's one already? I should really get to bed, Alex and I are supposed to get up early for a run in the morning. He's helping me train for a half marathon in a few weeks." He looks over to where Ash, Jake and Alex are playing what must be their twentieth game of pool. "They don't look in any rush to leave. Do you want me to give you a ride home?" he asks hesitantly.

I pause and follow his gaze to the pool table, mentally calculating how much longer I'd have to wait till they're done. Crap, it looks like they recently started a new game.

It's probably a bad idea, but I really don't feel like staying out much later. "Yeah, that would be great." I nod and lead him over to the group to say goodbye. "I'm heading home, Lucas is gonna give me a ride," I say.

Ash, Jake and Alex all look up at the same time—eyes wide, brows raised—with identical expressions. It's comical really.

I roll my eyes at them. "It's just a ride home," I mutter, glaring at them to knock it off.

Ash wipes the smirk off her face and gives me a kiss on the cheek. "Text me when you're home, okay?"

I assure her I will and follow Lucas out of the bar.

Lucas opens the car door for me, and I try to tamp down the warm rush in my chest. It rises back up with a vengeance once we're both settled in, and instead of starting the car he turns to face me. There's that flash of emotion moving across his face again. "Look, Lila. I really am sorry about what happened," he says, his eyes boring into mine.

"Let's not even get into it," I say gently, waving him off. It's too late and I'm too buzzed to have this conversation.

The look of vulnerability on his face throws me off guard. He breathes out a sigh but continues, "I really do feel terrible about it. I just want you to know that I know I should've handled things differently."

I shrug a shoulder and look out the window, prying my eyes from his penetrating gaze. "Really, it was so long ago. We were just kids then."

A discouraged sound escapes his lips. "Lila, look at me." He grabs my chin with his hand and turns my head.

As our gazes lock, all I can hear is the sound of my own racing heartbeat. All of a sudden the tension in this car is palpable. Once again, the years that have gone by disappear with a flash and I'm back in that pantry in high school. There's no denying the heat and attraction vibrating from both of us right now.

He moves his palm to cup my cheek and I automatically tilt my head, leaning into it. His thumb grazes the delicate skin under my eye. "You're so fucking beautiful," he whispers, his eyes tracking down my face to my lips.

We both lean in at the same time, like magnets being pulled toward each other. His lips lightly caress my own and I part them for him. He deepens the kiss, tongue sweeping against mine, and I unconsciously let out a moan. I reach my hands around his head and pull him even closer. I'm so lost in the kiss that I don't even realize what I'm doing.

"Shit, Lila..." He cradles my face in his hands and pulls back, breath shuddering. "I've thought about kissing you again for years."

I blush as my lips curve into a smile and I lean my forehead against his.

"Would you come home with me?" he asks softly, looking up at me through his lashes hesitantly. "We don't even have to do anything. I just don't want to leave you right now." He looks at me with such sincerity.

All my senses flew out the window the second I buckled my seatbelt. I nod my head yes, unable to control my grin.

He beams back at me, grabs my hand and starts to drive.

We get back to his house and it's just like I remember it—a split-level, clean and tidy, no clutter at all. It's taken on a bachelor-pad vibe: a large flat-screen on the wall, the black leather sofa, an absence of any decorative accents. Lucas tells me his mom moved to Arizona last year, leaving him the house. He gestures for me to take a seat on the couch and I oblige as he disappears into the kitchen. My stomach twists as the doubt starts to creep in. *What am I doing?* Is this a smart decision? I really hope this doesn't backfire in my face. I wring my hands as I sink back into the sofa, trying to calm the panic spiking inside of me.

He walks back in, hands me a beer and takes a sip of his own as he sits next to me. My heart constricts as our legs touch and his eyes slide to mine. His expression betrays his own nerves as I notice the stiffness in his posture and tightness in his jaw. He puts the beer on the table and reaches out to rest his hand on my thigh, a nervous smile on his lips. I turn toward him and try to calm my hammering heart.

His eyes shine with amusement as he lets out a laugh, breaking the tension. "You can relax. I promise we really don't have to do anything. I just couldn't take you home. We can watch some TV?" he asks, sensing my unease.

I love how perceptive he is, but I do want to do this. I've wanted to do this my whole life. I try to relax my shoulders and swallow my nerves. I reach out and touch his bottom lip with my thumb.

He looks startled at first, but quickly recovers and gently kisses the pad of my finger, taking the tip between his lips. His eyes bore into mine as I see the same flash of lust I saw in the car. He must see the same heat in my own gaze, because before I know it he's lifted me onto his lap so I'm straddling him. His lips crash into mine as I reach behind him and run my fingers through the back of his hair. We're all lips and tongue and teeth and I can't get enough of him. As the kiss goes on we're both panting for breath, neither of us willing to come up for air.

I feel his hardness underneath me and I start rocking against him, too turned-on and caught up in how incredible he feels to be embarrassed by how much I want him right now. He trails a line of kisses across my jaw and down my neck, dragging his tongue across my collarbone, driving me wild. I start to really grind my hips against his, deepening the intensity of my movements.

"Fuck, Lila," he groans as he lifts my tank top off in one swoop. He pulls down the straps of my bra and kisses my breasts. "You're so fucking beautiful," he says, looking up at my face.

I let out my own moan as he teases my nipple with his tongue. "I want you. Now," I say to him.

"Yes ma'am." His mouth lifts into a smirk and he stands up with me still straddling him. I giggle and my legs tighten around his waist as he walks down the hall to his room. It thrills me how easily he can carry me. I wrap my arms around his neck and lean in to kiss the tender spot below his ear. His breath hitches and his grasp on my butt tightens. My arousal intensifies with his body's reaction to me.

He tosses me down on the bed and reaches up behind him to pull his own shirt off.

God, that was sexy. I bite down on my lower lip.

"The way you look at me kills me." He lets out a low growl as he unbuttons my pants and tugs them off, sliding his hands up and down my thighs. "Where do you want me to touch you?" he asks with a glint in his eye.

"Everywhere," I breathe out as I arch my back in anticipation.

He teases circles down my torso and around my belly

button until he reaches the edge of my underwear. "You want me to touch you here?" he asks as he presses a finger against the material.

I'm incoherent at this point, and he laughs at my failure to respond. I squirm underneath him and grab the sheets in my fists. He tugs my undies to the side and slips a finger inside me as he kisses the inside of my thigh. I almost completely fall apart right there. He trails his tongue slowly up and down my inner thighs as he works me with his finger until I can't take it any longer.

"I need you inside me now," I whimper as I reach down and grab his arms, dragging him up to me.

His face splits into a knowing grin and he leans over me, reaching into his bedside table drawer and pulling out a condom.

I look down as he puts it on and bite back a laugh as I remember Ash joking about his penis curving to the left in high school. *Well she was certainly wrong about that*, I think with a grin.

"What's so funny?" he asks, eyes dancing at me. I shake my head, still smiling, and cinch my legs around him, pulling him over me. "I've thought about this moment so many times," he says, looking down into my eyes right before he enters me. We both let out a long moan as soon as he's inside. I wrap my arms around his muscular shoulders, drawing him closer. I rock my hips up to meet his thrusts, and I let my head fall back as we fall into a rhythm. It's like he's inside my head, anticipating my every need before I even realize it myself. I'm completely and utterly consumed by him.

He reaches out to grab hold of the headboard and his piercing green eyes bore into mine with such intensity, never breaking contact. It adds a whole new layer of intimacy and eroticism that I've never experienced. I've also thought about this moment a million times, I have dreamed about it for what feels like my entire life. The way our bodies seem inherently familiar to each other makes me believe it was destined to happen.

"Fuck, Lila, I'm not gonna last much longer," he groans. He feels so good, I quickly begin to climb myself, and I call out his name as the last shudder leaves me breathless. His release follows shortly after, and he sucks in air, trying to still his quaking body. We're both panting, sweat slicking our skin.

He hovers over me and kisses the tip of my nose. "That was amazing," he says, lying down next to me.

Holy shit, that was amazing indeed. I've never felt anything like that before. I turn to face him and smile in agreement.

He lets out a sigh and closes his eyes. He's so beautiful up close, his dark lashes fanning his cheeks, his square jaw, his lips slightly parted. I could just lay here and stare at him forever, basking in the afterglow of what just transpired. I feel a warm hum running through my body. My mind is still catching up, still processing what just happened between us.

He senses me staring and reaches his arms around me and pulls me into him. I rest my head on his chest and breathe in his Lucas smell. He pulls the comforter over us both and I listen to every breath he takes as they get longer and more drawn out as he falls into sleep. I try to fight it off as best I can so I can enjoy a few more moments before exhaustion eventually overcomes me as well.

CHAPTER 10

I hear a lawn mower. Crap, it's loud. It feels like a jackhammer beating my skull, and I wince as I try to force my eyes open through what feels like sandpaper. I manage to pry one open and I see an unfamiliar room. *Where the hell am I?* It all comes flooding back to me. I'm in Lucas's bed! That's his arm draped around my waist! That's him breathing next to me! I don't feel any clothes on my body. *Holy shit, we had sex last night!*

I feel a rush of giddiness as the memories form through the fog in my pounding head. I can't believe I actually had sex with Lucas. If only my twelve-year-old self could see me now. My joy is quickly squashed by a wave of anxiety as I register how bad my hangover is. How drunk was I, exactly? I may have had one too many beers at the bar, and then I remember another one when we got back here. I hope I didn't embarrass myself. Thankfully I remember every detail; I would be so disappointed if after all this time, I finally got my moment with Lucas to only black out and not even remember it.

I inwardly groan when I realize I also never texted Ash when I got home. I wonder if they know I slept here. Is Jake going to go apeshit again? My dread intensifies as I play the worst-case scenario card in my head. What time is it, anyway? I try to gauge from the sunlight streaming through the window, but it's hard to tell in summer. My eyes float around the room till they land on the time illuminated on the cable box. 8:16 a.m. *Shit!*

I jump up as panic fills my chest, suddenly remembering that Alex was supposed to come by early to get Lucas for a run. He cannot see me here, a naked disaster in Lucas's bed. "Shit, shit, shit!" I mutter, and tear through the debris of clothes and pillows on the floor looking for my underwear.

Lucas moans. "Morning," he rasps out. "What time is it?" His hand reaches out to find his phone on the night table.

"*OhmygodLucasgetup!*" I manage to squeak out while tugging one arm through my bra. "Isn't Alex coming like right now?" *Crap, crap, crap.*

Lucas sits up, rubbing his eyes. "Actually, he's late. He was supposed to be here at eight," he says, looking at his phone. He scrubs a hand down his face and back up over his head, leaving a trail of hair sticking every which way. If I wasn't in such a tailspin, I would stop and admire how adorable he is in the morning. All I can think about in this moment is finding my fucking underwear.

Remembering my tank top is on the couch, I manage to collect the rest of my clothes scattered around the room and shimmy into my jeans before I catch a glimpse of myself in the mirror above the dresser. I let out a little yelp; I look like a goddamn horror show. Mascara has run down my face and my hair is a rats' nest on my head. And not in an adorable way like Lucas's.

He looks over at me, startled, and a laugh escapes his lips when he sees my expression.

I fall back on the bed and throw my hands over my face. "This is not happening," I half laugh, half cry. I'm way too hungover for this crap right now. And I would die for a cup of fucking coffee.

"Lila, look at me." He leans over and pries my hands from my eyes. "Last night was amazing. You look beautiful." He kisses the tip of my nose.

I scoff at him. "Yeah, sure I do. Can you please get up before we get busted? *Again*." I sit up, grab my phone and open the Uber app. Oh thank you *Jesus*, there's one six minutes away. I blow out a sigh and say a quick prayer of gratitude, thankful there's not a long wait for my walk-of-shame ride home right now.

Lucas gets up and kneels down in front of me, palming my knees with his hands, and looks me in both eyes. "Lila, relax. You just graduated college. We aren't kids anymore. You're a grown woman. You can make your own decisions." He reaches up and tugs a strand of my hair and puts it behind my ear, smoothing it down.

I roll my eyes at him. "You want Alex to see me like this?" I gesture down the length of my body from my bedhead to my practically naked torso, brows raised at him.

He cocks his head and bites his lip, considering my point.

I really have to get out of here. I stand up and start frantically wiping the black eye makeup from under my eyes.

Lucas yawns and stretches, his six pack on full

display. For fuck's sake, he looks photoshopped. I blush as memories from last night come rushing back. He catches my eye and smirks, knowing full well what I'm thinking. I cover my face with my hands again.

He laughs and envelops me in a hug, tucking my head under his chin. "Can you chill, please? It's gonna be okay," he tries to assure me.

I shake my head against his chest. "I have to go." I extract myself from his large, muscular frame and open his bedroom door. I make a mad dash to the living room and fish my tank out of the sofa cushions. Thank God he lives alone; I could not deal with any kind of roommate situation right now. Or worse, his mother. I'm dreading the next part of this walk of shame into my own house. I pray Jake is still sleeping when I get home. Better yet, maybe he's still out—having hooked up himself—and is waking up in some girl's bed right now. *Ew, Lila.* I shudder at the thought. Still, I hope his exit is more graceful than mine.

I practically trip myself in the hallway as I pull my shoes on my feet on the way to the front door. My hand is on the knob when I hear knocking on the other end. I quickly duck, my heart in my throat.

Lucas bursts out laughing behind me. "Lila, what the hell are you doing?" He's looking at me like I'm crazy.

"Shhh!" I whisper-shout as I peek out the glass panel.

"Yo, Luke. Open up!" Alex's muffled voice calls through the door.

"This is so not ideal," I moan, flattening myself against the wall, willing my heart to stop hammering in my chest. I know I'm probably overreacting right now, but I just can't bear the thought of Alex having a front-row seat to the morning after my very first night with Lucas.

Lucas shakes his head at me and reaches out to turn the knob as I scurry into the corner to hide. He opens it up a quarter and pokes his head out. "Sorry bro, I overslept. Give me two minutes," he says, motioning for Alex to wait on the porch, and scurries back down the hall.

"No worries, man. I gotta pee real quick anyway." Alex pushes the door open the rest of the way and steps into the foyer. He spots me huddling in the corner and lets out a startled yelp, his hand flying to his chest. "Holy shit, Lila, you gave me a fucking heart attack!" He bends over with his hands on his thighs, trying to recover.

I groan and sink to the floor, hiding my face in my hands.

His eyebrows skyrocket as the realization dawns. "Um, did you sleep here?" he asks. "I *knew* it! When you two left together last night I just *knew* it!" He says it victoriously, pumping his fist.

I study his face through my fingers. He doesn't seem mad, he seems amused. He's smirking at me. He kind of looks like he's making fun of me, actually. I'm not sure what to do. I stay frozen on the floor and don't say a word. Maybe he'll just go away.

"Can you get out of that corner, you weirdo." He reaches down and pulls me up by my elbows.

Lucas comes back down the hallway holding his running shoes. He still looks entertained by my dramatics, but has one eye on Alex, carefully assessing his reaction as well.

"I was never here," I squeak out, wrapping my arms around myself.

Alex snorts and backs away with his hands up. "Oh, I'm staying out of it this time," he says. "I just came here for my running buddy. I didn't see anyone, I don't know anything and I'm just going to pee." He points in the direction of the bathroom and disappears out of sight.

Still momentarily stuck in place, my gaze slides to Lucas.

His face splits into a grin. "Now was that so bad?" he asks, gesturing to where Alex was standing.

I peek down the hallway to the bathroom then turn back to look at him. "Not exactly how I always pictured it," I say with a sigh.

I hear a car turn in the driveway. Finally. *Thank you, Uber gods!* I give Lucas a quick peck on the cheek and fling myself out the door to the safety of my ride, praying I didn't leave a trail of belongings behind.

Luckily, when I get home I manage to tiptoe inside my house and up to my room without seeing anyone. Jake's door is closed, so I figure he's still sleeping. I wonder how late they all stayed out. I have two missed calls from Ash, but I'm so tired and my head is still pounding, so I decide to call her back later. I climb into bed, hoping to catch a couple more hours of sleep. I must drift off immediately because I'm dreaming about last night and Lucas dragging his tongue down my body when all of a sudden I'm being shaken awake.

"Lila, wake up. Hello? Are you in there?" Ash is sitting on my bed shaking my shoulder, pulling me out of a deep sleep.

I jolt upright, almost knocking her on the floor. "What is it, Ash? What's wrong?" My heart is racing, thinking there must be some kind of emergency.

She laughs. "Nothing's wrong—relax." She holds out her hands, trying to calm me from her perch on my bed. "But you need to get up. *We're going to the beach!*" She sings this last part.

"What? No way, Ash. Traffic will be a bitch today." The beach? Is she crazy? I'm not facing holiday weekend traffic to sit on a mobbed Jones Beach for a few hours. Especially not with this hangover. I lay back on the pillows and throw an arm over my face. I groan and flick her hand away when she starts shaking me again, my headache returning with a vengeance.

"No, Li, not Jones. Montauk! We're going for the weekend. Come on, get up—you have to pack. Where the hell have you been, anyway?" She gets up and flings open my closet door. "Did you sleep here last night? I've been calling you all morning," she adds with a knowing glance.

I sit back up, confused, ignoring her question. "Huh? Montauk? Really?"

Her mouth quirks with amusement at my string of one-word questions. "Yes. Montauk. Really. The guys' friend, Thomas, has a share-house out there and some people pulled out last minute. So he offered the rooms to Jake this morning. It's apparently a whole finished basement. Right in Ditch Plains! Alex is driving. And we're leaving ASAP." She claps her hands at me, gesturing to get up as she moves on from my closet to my dresser.

I frown and rub my eyes. She's awfully fucking chipper today. *And loud.* It's taking me a minute to process this information through the haze in my brain. I'm assuming "the guys" means my brother and Alex?

"Wait, how exactly do you know this?" I eye her skeptically as she rifles through my bikini drawer.

She doesn't seem to hear me; she's laser-focused on my swimsuits. "Where is that black bandeau with the open back? I know it's in here somewhere," she murmurs. She tosses a handful of rejects on the floor and keeps on digging, completely ignoring my question.

"Um, hello Ashley? How exactly do you know this information?" I press on, my voice getting louder as I try to pry her attention back to me.

She shrugs a bony shoulder. "Jake told me. We went for a run this morning. Which brings me back to my previous question, missy: Where have you been? You never texted me last night. Did you sleep at Lucas's?" She finally pauses her bikini hunt to give me the side-eye from across the room, accusation lacing her tone.

I scoff at the mention of more physical activity, and now it's my turn to purposely avoid *her* question. "Why is everyone going for a run at the buttcrack of dawn? Is nobody else hungover?" I moan as I grab my head between my hands and sink back down into my fluffy pillows.

"Are you going to answer my question? Better yet, are you going to get up and start packing? Pack and talk, pack and talk." She whips the comforter off me and motions her hands for me to get moving.

I get up with a huff and lay the comforter back in its place over my bed. She's back in my closet now, pulling stuff off of hangers. I push her aside and kneel to fish out my overnight bag from way in the back. Jeez, talk about last-minute plans.

Finally yanking the bag free, I pause for a breath and turn to her. "Are we really going to Montauk right now?" I ask as I try to push through my hangover fog and run down the list of what I'll need for a weekend at the beach.

"And who exactly is coming, anyway?" It dawns on me that I have no idea who I'm agreeing to share a house with for the weekend.

"Me, you, Jake, Alex, Lucas." She ticks off her fingers with each name. "And that guy Thomas and his girlfriend will be there, obviously. And a few other people that I don't know."

I swing around to face her, my eyes wide at the mention of his name. "Lucas is coming?"

She pauses for a beat, studying my face. "You dirty stay-out! I *so* knew it when you didn't text me when you got home last night," she says with a smirk.

My cheeks heat up, and I'm unable to do anything but continue to gawk at her.

"Spill. Now," she demands, cocking her head with impatience.

I purse my lips. "I might have slept at Lucas's..." I trail off. My face splits into a broad smile. I duck my head and let my hair fall over my face.

"Um, what?" she yells, indignant. "That's all I get? 'I might have slept at Lucas's'? You finally sleep with the love of your life and that's how you tell your *best friend*?" she says in mock protest, eyes wide.

"Okay, okay, sorry!" I put my hands up in surrender, which she grabs with both of hers and shakes them with a grin. I laugh at her excitement. I guess being my best friend for twenty years, she's invested in this milestone as well. "Yes, we slept together," I confirm with a nod.

She wiggles her brows. "And?"

"And, it was nice," I admit, my smile growing even wider.

She rolls her eyes at me and snorts, repeating my words back again. "It was 'nice'?"

"Okay," I relent. "It was amazing. Everything I always thought it would be and more." I bite my lip as I remember just how amazing, then wince at the dramatics that followed this morning. "Until Alex showed up early today for a *run*," I add, giving her a pointed look. "He caught me hiding in a corner looking like a hot mess." I wrinkle my nose as the memory sharpens my embarrassment.

An incredulous laugh escapes her. "Wait, what?"

I cover my face with my hands. "It was mortifying. He bursts into the house literally two seconds after I pull on my clothes. He sees me ducking behind the door, which apparently scares the shit out of him." I pause and look up for effect. "Yup, apparently *I* startled *him*, and then I ran out into my Uber." I grimace as the whole scene replays in my mind. Worst walk of shame ever.

She gapes at me. "Wow. I don't even know what to say about that."

I nod. "Brutal."

"So what does this mean for you guys? What happens now?" she asks, always one step ahead.

I shake my head and shrug. "I have no idea, but there is no way I'm getting my hopes up this time. It was probably just his way of apologizing. He kept saying how bad he felt about what happened in high school. Who knows, but this is going to be so awkward in a car for three hours, Ash! I'm serious when I said I bolted out of there. Both of them must think I'm nuts," I wail at her. I put a hand on my chest as a swirl of anxiety runs through me.

She laughs. "Well you're gonna find out really soon, since they're coming in like fifteen minutes."

And with another jolt of panic, I start packing faster.

Sure enough, fifteen minutes later Alex is outside honking the horn.

"Lila, Ash, are you ready? Let's go," Jake yells from downstairs.

My stomach flips and I impulsively grab a floppy sun hat from my closet to hide behind.

We carry our bags outside where the guys are cramming everything in the trunk of Alex's Jeep. I use the hat as a shield to cover my face, the coward that I am. Alex grins to himself when he sees me, struggling to hold in a laugh. I shoot him a death glare. I pray he stuck to his word and didn't say anything to Jake about this morning. I don't need everyone else knowing about it yet.

Lucas catches my eye and gives me his signature Lucas smile. Just seeing that smile directed at me is enough to send my pulse into overdrive. My thoughts are hijacked by images of us last night in his bed. I blush and look away, ducking even more under my hat.

I look over at Jake, who's preoccupied with shoving a cooler in the car with a goofy grin on his face. Interesting. Wonder what's got him so happy? Maybe he did hook up last night after all. I scan my memory for faces of girls we saw last night, racking my brain for possibilities. I come up empty, only able to remember how Lucas's t-shirt displayed his biceps perfectly. And how he ripped said t-shirt off his torso when we got home.

I'm pulled from my daydream as Jake finally gets the trunk shut and yells, "Shotgun!" before making a dash for the front passenger seat. I sigh and tell myself to get my shit together.

"To the beach we go!" Alex says, getting in and starting the car.

Ash opens the back door and turns to face me. I

freeze, knowing what's coming next. "Lila, you get middle. You know I get carsick." She motions with her hand for me to get in first.

I stare at her, eyes wide, hoping she'll at the very least have mercy on my hangover, if not the fact that I made a fool of myself this morning. I really can't be smushed against Lucas for three hours in the back of this car.

She offers an apologetic smile as she lifts her shoulder into a shrug that conveys no mercy will be had.

"Lucky me," I mutter as I hop in and scoot to the middle. I take a steadying breath, reminding myself to be happy that we're going to the beach for the weekend. I should also be relieved that nobody has mentioned a word about last night. Yet. This ride is long, so I really hope it stays that way. Anything can happen in three hours.

Lucas silently climbs in next to me while I busy myself with the seatbelt. His warm thigh presses against mine and the butterflies are back. I try not to breathe. His hand finds mine and he gives my fingers a squeeze. I see his mouth quirk out of the corner of my eye, and I slowly let out the breath I was holding. I'm obviously thrilled to be going on vacation with him after last night—but at the same time, I'm also terrified to be going on vacation with him after last night. One of my biggest dreams has just come true, and I haven't had any time to process it yet. Ideally, I would be doing it without an audience.

"Put on some tunes, J," Ash calls to my brother. I try to relax as Jake turns the radio up, obliging her. I close my eyes and lean my head back against the seat, settling into the three-hour drive ahead, still holding Lucas's hand.

Surprisingly, the holiday traffic isn't terrible and we make great time, hitting the stretch after Amagansett on Montauk Highway right before 3 p.m. As soon as I see the familiar scenery and breathe in the salty air, my hangover seems to disappear. My family has been coming to Montauk in the summers since I was young, and it always has a calming effect on me. My favorite part of the long trip is when you come over the hill from the highway and get that first glimpse of the ocean glittering under the sun, stretching out into the horizon.

The town is busy—no surprise there, being July Fourth weekend—so it takes a good ten minutes for Alex to maneuver through all the crawling cars and tourists on foot. We navigate to the Ditch Plains community just past the main stretch of town and pull up to an amazing two-story house just a few blocks from the beach. The house has a wrap-around porch on each story and looks like it belongs on *Million Dollar Listing*. Alex pulls into the wide gravel driveway next to two other cars, and we all gape at our surroundings, speechless.

"Whose house is this again?" I ask in awe.

"You remember Thomas, he was on our hockey team," Alex reminds me. "This is his share with a few buddies of his from college."

"Wow," says Ash with an excited squeak as she unbuckles her seatbelt and jumps out of the car.

Lucas opens his door and offers his hand to help me down. He regards me silently with amused eyes as he stretches his arms over his head. He fell asleep about twenty minutes into the trip, so I managed to avoid any awkwardness. I tried to follow suit, but I couldn't stop my whirling brain from overanalyzing every little detail from last night and this morning. I also got a few knowing smirks from Alex in the rearview mirror the few times I did open my eyes.

At this point, last night almost feels like a dream.

Lucas doesn't seem to regret it, and I definitely don't either, but I don't want to get pulled down the rabbit hole of Lucas for it all to blow up in my face. Again. I'm walking into this cautiously this time, with both eyes open. There's also Jake to consider—I do not want to repeat our mistake with my brother, no matter how mature and over high school he seems to be.

As the guys are hauling our bags out of the car, a guy I instantly recognize as Thomas comes out to welcome us wearing swim trunks and his hair wet from the pool. He looks the same as he did in high school—stocky, boyish smile, cute. A girl about my age follows him out, also in a swimsuit, and he introduces her as Lucy, his girlfriend.

After the usual dude hug/pound scenario with the guys, Thomas leans down to grab a duffel from the growing pile on the ground and hauls it over his shoulder. "I'm so glad you could make this work last minute," he says to us. "The rest of the crew is still at the beach but should be back soon. We're going to BBQ here for dinner and then have a bonfire back at the beach later tonight. Come on, I'll give you the tour." He motions for us to follow him into the house.

My jaw drops as soon as I step over the threshold. The house is even more amazing inside. The whole main level is an open-living concept with the back wall entirely made of glass so you can see out to the pool. A huge, modern kitchen flows into the living room and dining room. The walls and floors are white, as is most of the furniture, and the decor is beachy with a nautical theme— tasteful shell and anchor accents scattered throughout. The sliding glass doors lead out to a beautiful stone patio underneath a trellis of twinkly lights. There's a state-of-the-art grilling area equipped with its own sink and a large round table with an umbrella off to the side. Just beyond the patio is a sparkling blue pool with a running waterfall from the hot tub perched above the far corner, and a row of very comfortable-looking cushioned lounge chairs.

"Let me take you down to where you guys will be crashing so you can change and get settled," Thomas says. "Put on your suits and come meet us out back by the pool. I'm sure you're itching for a drink after that drive."

Ash has to pry me away from gawking through the glass at the exquisite backyard as he leads us downstairs. The finished basement is enormous and is equipped with a pool table, a giant flat screen on the wall and two pull-out sofas. There are also two small additional bedrooms and a bathroom. You can sleep eight down here, easily. This basement is bigger than my parents' whole house.

Ash and I claim one of the rooms for ourselves, and we quickly change into our bikinis. I don't even know what I packed this morning, but thankfully I threw a matching swim set in my bag. I did, however, forget a cover-up in my haste. After dumping all my stuff out on the bed and rummaging through it, Ash reads my mind and hands me a tank dress of hers.

"What would I do without you?" I say.

She gives me a knowing grin. "I figured I'd pack some extra stuff for you given your state of disarray earlier. Which, by the way, I'm still waiting for details about," she says as she steps into a pair of cut-off shorts.

"Later," I promise her. "Do you think Jake knows? Is it obvious?" I ask, pulling the dress over my head.

"You mean from the three hours in the car you guys spent with your eyes closed? No, I don't think that gave anything away," she says sarcastically.

I snort at the truth of her words. "It's like I totally forgot how to act like a human all of a sudden," I say and sit on the bed. "I think I'm still in shock. This is all so sudden. I didn't even want to go out last night! I haven't talked to him since he broke my heart in high school, and I just gave it up like nothing ever happened. I don't know what to think right now, Ash. Do you think he thinks it was a mistake? Was it a mistake? I can't go through a heartbreak like that again." I drop my head into my hands. Dread pools in my belly as I remember the sting of first love gone wrong, and the anxious thoughts whir through my head.

She sits down next to me and takes my hand. "Li, we're grownups now. You're no longer a kid in high school, okay? You are a smart, beautiful college graduate. We both are, for that matter." She tosses her hair over her shoulder, and I chuckle at her as she continues. "You're the one who gets to call the shots. Forget what he thinks, or what Jake thinks. Do *you* think it was a mistake?" she asks, her tone serious now.

I study the carpet as I consider her question. "No, I don't think it was a mistake. Being with him just feels right, like everything clicks into place. Last night it was like we were the only two people in the world." As the words leave my mouth, I feel the gravity of their truth.

"Well then, there's your answer." She smiles at me and gives my leg a reassuring pat.

Jake knocks on the door. "Are you girls decent?"

"Yep, what's up?" I ask as he peeks his head in.

"Let's go get in that pool!" He opens the door wider so he can whip his towel at Ashley.

She yelps and chases after him.

I laugh and follow them out of the room, almost

bumping into Lucas in the hallway. He's wearing light-blue swim trunks and a white t-shirt and looks sexy as hell. I should really buy stock in his brand of white tees.

"Hi," he says, smiling down at me.

I look around; we're the only two left downstairs. "Hi." I smile back and clear my throat. "Um, about this morning..." I trail off, unable to formulate words.

"Don't worry about it," he says when he sees me struggling. "I get it. Last night took me by surprise, too."

"Yeah, I wasn't expecting that to happen." My cheeks grow hot at the memory.

"But I'm glad it did." He leans down to touch his lips lightly to mine.

I smile against his mouth. "Me too," I say as I open my eyes to meet his gaze.

"I'm glad to hear that. I'm not gonna lie, I got a little nervous at how fast you hightailed it away from me this morning."

I wince and shift my weight. "I know, I'm sorry. Alex completely unnerved me. Add in the hangover and I momentarily lost my mind," I admit sheepishly. "What did he say when I left?"

"He said it's none of his business, but if I hurt you again he'll rip my balls off." His face cracks into a wide grin.

"Sounds about right." I nod, snorting at Alex's words. "Do you think Jake knows?"

"Something tells me Jake is preoccupied," he says, lifting a brow as we hear Ashley screeching outside.

I take a beat as his meaning sinks in. "No way." Ash and Jake? I shrug the thought off.

He laughs and leans down to kiss me again. I forget what we're talking about. This time I wrap my arms around his neck and pull him closer. He sighs into my lips. "You're killing me."

Ash screeches again, and we both grin at the interruption. I remember his words and take a step back to consider them. He regards me with amusement as I chew my lip and try to wrap my head around Ashley being the girl to put that grin on my brother's face.

"Come on, let's go see what the racket is about," I say and take his hand to lead him up the stairs.

We make our way outside to the back, and sure enough Jake is tossing Ash around in the pool. They're giggling at each other like teenagers. Lucas gives me a knowing glance but doesn't say a word. This is so odd, but there's no denying that this is indeed some form of flirting. Thomas gets up from the patio table where he's sitting with Alex and Lucy and asks Lucas if he wants to accompany him on a quick beer run.

Lucas agrees and follows him back into the house.

I lower myself into the newly vacated seat next to Alex, and he offers me a beer. I grab it with a grateful smile and decide to just rip off the Band-Aid. I lean in and whisper to him, "Are we going to discuss this morning?"

"I have no idea what you mean." He smirks at me sideways. "I didn't see anything." He takes a pull of his beer.

I make a face and nod, feeling my cheeks heat up. "Okay then."

He chuckles and knocks my elbow with his own. "*Love is in the air*," he sings under his breath, his eyes twinkling.

I chug half of my beer.

He raises his eyebrows, amused. "Pace yourself, we have a long weekend ahead."

I look up as a group of people walk into the yard and almost spit out my mouthful of beer. There, right in front of me, in the flesh, is my ex-boyfriend, Jamie.

Alex eyes me as I try to swallow through a choking fit. Apparently this is a thing I do when I see my exes now, some sort of involuntary choking stress response. I can feel my insides start to twist as my mind catches up to what my eyes are seeing.

"Jamie?" I manage to squeak out once I catch my breath. *A long fucking weekend is right.*

CHAPTER 11

Jamie's eyes go wide when he registers who just called his name. His expression mirrors what I'm guessing mine looks like right now as the group draws closer.

I slowly rise from my seat, still in shock.

"Lila?!" He leans in to hug me. "What are you doing here?"

"I'm here for the weekend," I answer, hugging him back.

He pulls back to study me, confusion clouding his expression. "Here, in this house?"

I nod. "My brother and Thomas are friends from high school," I explain, trying to smooth out my own facial expression. "What about you?"

"Lucy is my cousin," he says as he points in her direction. "She invited me for the weekend. I took the ferry over from Rhode Island this morning."

His cousin? Ferry? My eyebrows retreat into my hairline as I look over at Alex—who is intently watching this exchange—for confirmation that Rhode Island is indeed just a ferry ride away. Could that be possible? He reads the question in my eyes and slowly nods at me like I'm a fourth grader learning geography for the first time.

"Wow, small world," I say after a beat, struggling to keep my voice even. This is just my luck.

Jamie, on the other hand, is buzzing with excitement. "This is awesome. It's so good to see you." He squeezes my hand. "I've really missed you, Lila." He beams at me like I'm his long-lost puppy.

Unease builds in my chest. Again, I look over to Alex.

His eyebrows are raised at us, a knowing smirk forming on his lips. He knows all about Jamie, *and* he knows all about my night with Lucas. I can tell he's amused as his brain connects the dots. After a moment of silence in which my mind takes me down a rabbit hole of horrible scenarios playing out this weekend, Alex mercifully stands up and holds his hand out to introduce himself.

I'm jolted back to reality. "Oh, sorry. Alex, Jamie. Jamie, Alex. I forgot you two have never met," I stammer as I stand there wringing my hands.

Alex looks downright gleeful.

After shaking Alex's hand, Jamie introduces the rest of the group. There are two other guys, Billy and Greg, and Greg's girlfriend, Morgan. I manage to squeak out a hello and a small wave to them just as Ash and Jake emerge from the pool, wrapping towels around their dripping bodies. Ash's lips look blue; I'm not surprised— they've been in there for a while.

I watch as her eyes register our new guest. "Holy shit, Jamie?" she exclaims. They met a few times on her many visits to me at school. Not to mention all the photos I sent her of us over the years.

Jamie grins at her. "Hey Ash, good to see you. I would hug you but you look...wet." He laughs.

She stands there shivering, glancing back and forth between us. I can tell she's trying to gauge how I feel about this new development.

Jake puts his towel around her shoulders and rubs his hands up and down her arms. My eyes follow the movement, then travel back to her face. She blushes and averts her eyes from mine. Wow, I think Lucas could actually be right about this. There's definitely something going on here between them.

Again, I'm jolted out of my head and back to the present when Jake speaks.

"Hey man, I'm Jake, Lila's brother. Nice to finally meet you, sorry I never got the chance on my visits to DC."

"Likewise. Nice to finally meet Lila's big bro." Jamie reaches out to shake Jake's hand.

Ash's teeth are now starting to chatter, and I push aside my mental fog. "Ash, maybe you should go change into dry clothes?"

"Oh, right. Um, come with me?" She beckons for me to follow her downstairs.

I trail behind her into the house and down the steps to the basement, Jake hot on our heels. Once we reach the bottom step, she spins around to face me. "Holy shit," she says, eyes wide. I stop short, almost knocking right into her. "Holy shit," she repeats.

I step around her and walk into our room, craving some space to breathe.

"Why do you keep saying 'holy shit'?" I hear Jake ask her behind me.

I guess my brother really is clueless. Or he's just all of a sudden blinded by my best friend.

Ash ignores him and follows me into the room. "Are you okay?" she asks, concerned.

I gape at her, speechless, trying not to freak out. More than I am already, at least.

"Okay, well if nobody is going to tell me what's going on, I'm hopping in the shower," Jake says from the doorway, and disappears into the bathroom.

I sit on the bed and lean my elbows on my knees, sucking in a breath. "Whathefuck?" I breathe out with a groan.

She sits next to me and puts a hand on my back. "Okay, okay, don't freak out. It will be fine," she tries to assure me, but it comes out flat.

I snort at her. "Ugh, this is so not fine."

"Agreed, it's not ideal. This weekend has taken an interesting turn. Maybe Lucas won't even realize who he is. Where is he, anyway?"

"He went on a beer run with Thomas while you guys were in the pool." I eye her sideways. "What the hell is going on with the two of you, anyway?" I ask, getting sidetracked from my own personal dumpster fire.

She looks at me blankly and shrugs a bony shoulder, which is still dripping from her wet hair. "What? I don't know what you mean. Do you know when they're going to start the grill? I'm starving," she says, deflecting.

She gets up and starts rummaging through her cosmetics bag. "Come on, let me do your hair and makeup. Now you really gotta look hot tonight." She zips up a hoodie over her swimsuit and motions for me to move closer to her on the bed. She plugs in the curling iron and starts arranging hair products and makeup on the top of the dresser. Once the plethora of beauty products is unpacked, she starts applying them to my face.

"What do you think I should do?" I ask, forgetting about her convo pivot and jumping back to my own drama.

She stops dusting shadow on my lids and regards me carefully. "Well, that depends. Are you definitely over Jamie? And where do you think this is going with Lucas?"

I roll my eyes at her. "I have no idea, Ash! This all happened so fast. Like five minutes ago you guys were convincing me to leave my house to go to Catch, now all of a sudden I'm on vacation with my ex and my new whatever-he-is slash love of my life," I cry, and put my face in my hands.

"No touching your face!" She pulls my hands down and comes back at me with the eyeshadow brush.

I sigh and let her do my eyes, because let's face it, if I can at least look good maybe it'll give me the confidence I need to get through this weekend. "As awesome at makeup as you are, I don't think an extra layer of mascara is going to solve this for me," I say sullenly while she pokes and prods me.

She gives me a pointed look. "You'd be surprised what mascara can do."

"Um, Lila?" Alex pokes his head through the doorway, looking concerned. "You might want to get upstairs. Lucas just got back."

I freeze and look back and forth between them, my heart in my throat. "Shit."

Ash bites her lip.

Alex looks like he's trying not to laugh at my state of alarm as he steps into the room. "Who'd have thought little Lila would have two boyfriends in one house?" he teases me with a mocking grin.

I put my head back in my hands.

Ash slaps them away. "Do not mess up your makeup!"

"Okay, okay. This is okay." I get up and start pacing the room. "I'll just go upstairs and act like it's nothing, like Jamie is just a friend from school. Lucas never has to know he's my ex-boyfriend. Right? That sounds good, right?" I look at them for approval and groan as my own ridiculous words register in my head.

"You should probably just be honest," Alex chimes in with his words of wisdom.

"Be honest about what?" Jake chooses this moment to walk in from his shower with a towel around his waist. I notice Ashley's eyes scan the length of his body. *Ugh, gross.* I don't have the mental capacity to handle whatever is going on here on top of everything else.

The moment stretches; nobody says a word. I avert my eyes from all of them and sit back down on the bed.

Alex is suddenly very interested in all of Ash's makeup scattered on top of the dresser. Ash's eyes are still glued to my brother's naked torso.

"Okay, can someone please tell me what the hell is going on?" Jake asks impatiently as he pulls a t-shirt over his head.

Crickets.

He sighs. "Does this have something to do with Lucas and Lila?" he probes, head cocked.

Now my eyes shoot up to his. Busted.

"What? I'm not blind, you know," he says to me with a pointed look.

"Uhh, I think I'll go back upstairs and help start the grill." Alex quickly takes his leave.

Ash walks over to the closet, busying herself with picking out her outfit.

I'm momentarily at a loss for words. I don't know what I should say. Again, this literally just happened and I don't exactly want to blurt out that I had sex with his best friend last night. I'm not intentionally hiding it, but I'm not ready for any questions that may arise. Especially before Lucas and I can even work it out ourselves. Jake doesn't exactly seem ruffled by the idea of us together, but I remember all too well the sting of what happened in high school, and I *really* don't want a repeat.

My head is a whirl of thoughts and I try to formulate my response.

"Are you going to just ignore me?" he asks, throwing up his hands.

I grimace as he snaps me out of my trance.

He unexpectedly grins at me, shaking his head. "Lila, I don't care. We aren't in high school anymore. Obviously there's something between you guys that keeps pulling you back toward each other. And I'm not gonna be the one to stand in your way if you want to figure it out."

I raise my brows at him. Well, that's particularly mature. "Really?" I ask, my tone dubious. I'm a bit taken aback by his response.

"Yes. Really," he repeats with emphasis. "I already admitted years ago that I could have reacted better back then. If you really like each other, you should go for it." He shrugs.

I'm not sure I believe my ears. *"Go for it?"* I parrot.

He holds up a finger. *"But* I will say that I'm staying out of it. Completely, this time. I don't want to hear about it if things go south. You hear me?" His sharp gaze locks with mine, making sure I'm absorbing his words.

I give him a little salute. "Yup, copy that." I hear Ash chuckle to herself in the closet.

He hooks a thumb over his shoulder. "And it looks like things might be starting to take that turn, so why don't you get upstairs."

"Right. Good idea." I nod, rising from the bed. Ash turns from the closet and hands me a tank top—a small, encouraging smile on her face. I give her a nod of thanks and go change before heading back to whatever awaits me upstairs.

I find Lucas alone in the kitchen, stocking the fridge with beer. The food is all prepped and ready to go on platters, and I feel a twang of guilt for disappearing downstairs for so long and not helping with dinner. Through the glass doors, I see Jamie scraping off the grill and the rest of the group sitting around the set patio table.

I begin to help Lucas and reach down to pick up beers from the boxes and hand them to him. "How was town?" I ask.

"Packed. We waited in line at the beer store for like twenty minutes. It snaked halfway down the block. But we bumped into some other buddies of ours that invited us to a pool party for the Fourth." He opens a beer and hands it to me before opening one for himself.

"Oh great, that should be fun," I say, my tone a little too chipper. I take a long pull of my beer. So much for trying to act nonchalant.

He eyes me critically. "Everything okay?"

"Yep, great!" I try to convince him with a smile.

"Lila, can you bring the burgers out?" Alex yells from outside.

"Sure!" I call back.

With my best reassuring smile plastered on my face, I

Down to You

set my beer down and grab the platter of hamburger patties sitting on the counter. I walk outside and go to hand them to Alex when Jamie chimes in, "I'll take those."

He steps toward me and reaches out to take the platter. "Come keep me company while I grill." He grins at me and gestures to follow him.

I hesitate for a beat. I can't exactly refuse, so I oblige and accompany him at the grill. He rolls up the sleeves on his linen button-down and starts placing the burgers on the grates. My eyes sweep over his muscular forearms. He's definitely kept up his fitness routine. My gaze trails up his torso to his face. Summer has been kind to him so far. His skin is sunkissed from having spent the day at the beach, and his sandy blond hair is lightened with natural highlights from the sun. His long, dark lashes frame blue eyes which are brighter than usual with his signature glasses replaced by contacts. He catches me staring at him and his face splits into a grin. I feel heat creep up my neck and quickly look away.

"I can't believe it's only been a few months since I've seen you. Can you believe college is really over? Kind of scary, right? Seems like just yesterday we were doing beer bongs at the frat house," he says wistfully.

"Tell me about it," I agree. "Time is flying by." I shift my weight on my feet, anticipating a walk down memory lane I would rather not have right now.

"Remember the first party we went to a few days after we met? You amazed everyone with your flip-cup skills. You were a true force to be reckoned with." His smile reaches his eyes as he remembers our first of many games of flip cup.

I laugh, recalling the night he's referring to. "Ha.

117

Didn't you win longest keg stand that night? When I introduced you to my friends your shirt was soaked with beer." I grin at the memory, feeling my shoulders relax. The tension eases as we fall back into a familiar easy banter.

Jamie cracks up. "Oh man, I was trying so hard to impress you that night. I wound up passed out on my floor, and woke up with the worst hangover of my life for the second week of classes. Not a good look." He shakes his head, still chuckling.

We stand there reminiscing while he flips the burgers on the grill.

Lucas comes outside and walks over to us. "Lila, there you are. You left your beer inside," he says. I feel my body stiffen again as he hands me my drink. The knot in my stomach tightens and I momentarily freeze, not knowing what to say. We all stand there in silence as the moment stretches, but I don't seem to know how to introduce them.

Finally, I find my voice. "Oh, Lucas, um, have you met Jamie yet? He's Lucy's cousin. We also went to school together. We were just talking about our old college days," I blurt, a nervous smile on my lips.

"'You mean, as in last week?" Lucas jokes. "Nice to meet you, man." He reaches out to shake Jamie's hand.

"Likewise," Jamie says, offering him a small smile that doesn't quite reach his eyes. I can tell he's sizing Lucas up. "So how do you two know each other?" he asks, glancing back and forth between us. I never told him about Lucas, never wanting to replay the whole thing again out loud.

Lucas waits for me to answer, his eyes carefully studying my face.

"We grew up together," I say. "Lucas, Jake and Alex have been best friends since grade school."

"Kindergarten, actually," Lucas corrects me, taking a sip of his beer.

"Yeah, it's um, been forever." I glance around, feeling uncomfortable as hell, knowing they each can feel the tension coming off me in waves.

Jamie nods and turns his attention back to the burgers on the grill. Lucas gives me a weird look.

I shift my weight again and try to smooth out my facial expression. I have no idea how to navigate this situation and my awkwardness is making it a million times worse.

Fortunately, I'm saved when Ashley and Jake come out of the house. Ash must notice my pained face among our trio, and she makes a beeline over to us. She starts peppering Jamie with questions about his accounting job and his new apartment in Rhode Island. As the tension in the air eases, so does my anxiety, but I know I can't avoid telling them about each other forever.

CHAPTER 12

After dinner, we walk the few blocks over to the beach for the bonfire. Jake and Ashley run ahead to the water while the rest of the group picks a spot on the sand and starts setting it up.

Lucas takes my hand and keeps going. "Let's go for a walk." He leads me down the beach, the waves lapping at our feet with our toes in the surf. There are a few groups of people around fires peppered down the shore.

After a few minutes of walking in comfortable silence, he stops at a large piece of driftwood. "Sit with me," he says, and pulls me onto his lap. I get a fluttery feeling in my chest as I flash back to high school and that first party at John's where we sat on the lounge chair together after winning beer pong. I laugh quietly to myself as the memory forms in my mind. That was the turning point of my childhood crush, the night the fantasy jumped out of my mind and into reality.

"What's so funny?" he asks, studying me curiously.

"Nothing, just remembering something from high school," I say, waving off the memory.

"Tell me," he probes.

"It's silly really. I was just thinking about my first senior party and how thrilled I was to finally be hanging out with you."

He looks at me with amusement. "Really?"

I give him the side-eye. "Oh stop. You know how I felt about you."

He shakes his head. "I really didn't. Well, not to that extent. Not until that last year, at least. I was a dumb teenager. Totally blind to what was right in front of me," he says. "And then I messed it all up," he adds quietly.

I turn to face him. "*We* messed it all up." Then jokingly add, "But really, Jake messed it all up." I grin at him, trying to lighten the mood.

He's not laughing; his face is somber. "No, this isn't on Jake. I should've handled it better. And I definitely shouldn't have just cut and run when things got hard. That wasn't fair to you. I feel terrible when I think about how abandoned you must have felt. I know how much you liked to hang out with us and how much we meant to you. I truly am sorry for being such a coward." His tone is laced with remorse.

While I appreciate his sincerity, I'm not in the mindset for a heart-to-heart right now. "Water under the bridge," I say lightly, and put my arm around his shoulder.

He leans in and presses his lips lightly against mine. I smile against his mouth. A big wave splashes our legs, surprising us both, and I jump out of his lap, yelping.

He laughs at me as he stands up and envelops me in a hug. "Let's do something just us tomorrow," he whispers in my ear.

"Okay," I agree, grinning. I tilt my head up for one last kiss before we make our way back to the group.

We slowly walk back side by side, enjoying the sound of the waves crashing on the shore. As we get closer to the group, we see Jamie and Thomas throwing a football back and forth down the beach.

"So how well do you know Jamie, anyway?" he asks me. My shoulders tense up as unease creeps down my spine. Crap, I knew this was coming. I pause, and my brain takes off spinning as I try to quickly decide on an answer. Do I spill mine and Jamie's whole history? Do I tell him he's just a friend?

He senses my hesitation and stops walking. He turns to face me, eyeing me critically.

I shrug and try to sound nonchalant. "I mean, we hung out a lot in college," I finally say, trying to keep it vague. I don't want him to feel threatened in any way, not so soon after I just got him back.

He arches a brow, giving me a skeptical look. "It looked like a bit more than just 'hanging out' to me, Li," he says pointedly.

"Okay, we may have hooked up a few times," I confess. "But that's all in the past!" My eyes slide to his face, gauging his reaction. It's hard to tell in the dusky light, but I can make out the hard set of his jaw. I inwardly groan; I really don't want anything to mess this up. I still can't believe Jamie is even here right now. Both of their alpha-male energy is a lot to handle. Things are going so well with Lucas, the last thing I need is him engaging in a pissing contest with my ex. We're finally getting a second chance here.

"And you had no idea he was going to be here?" he asks me, eyes tight with tension.

"No, of course not! I haven't even spoken to him since

graduation, Lucas. Really," I say vehemently, shaking my head.

That seems to placate him somewhat. He nods and continues walking. We reach our group around the fire and take a seat in two empty beach chairs next to Alex.

He catches my eye and silently asks me if everything is okay.

I give him my best reassuring smile, hoping it hides my nerves. While I'm relieved that Lucas dropped the subject for now, something tells me that won't be the last of the discussion.

On Alex's other side, Jake and Ash are canoodling in their own little bubble. It looks like he's teasing her and she slaps him playfully, then he reaches out and pokes her in the side, making her laugh and squirm into him. As I watch them, I realize how cute they look together. I wonder if they always felt an attraction to each other or if this is a completely new development. I make a mental note to ask Ash later if she always had a crush on him. If she did, I honestly had no idea—she did a good job hiding it all these years.

I sit back in my chair and watch the fire snap, crackle and pop and think about what a strange turn the last two days have taken. Literally yesterday at this time I had no idea I would be on the beach in Montauk, cuddled up to Lucas around a bonfire with my ex-boyfriend a few feet away. Crazy what a plot twist life has thrown at me in twenty-four hours.

Speaking of plot twists, Jamie and Thomas come over and join the group. Jamie's eyes snap to Lucas and me and instantly narrow, pinching his expression. He continues to study us as he takes a seat across the fire. I can't help but notice the rigid set to his shoulders and the flat line of his lips. My eyes connect with his and I shrink back under his penetrating gaze.

The conversation turns to plans for the Fourth of July. Ideas are thrown around on how we can celebrate. Thomas suggests we throw a party at the house, and Lucas reminds him about the party we were invited to earlier by their friends at the beer store.

"We saw this beer-pong float that would be pretty great for the pool," Thomas says, gesturing in Lucas's direction. "Maybe we should go back tomorrow and get it."

My ears perk up at the prospect of drinking games.

Lucas senses my excitement and grins at me. "Yeah that thing looked awesome, but we can also just set up a folding table and not risk getting beer in the pool."

"Well, whatever you do, don't let Lila play," Ash interjects.

"Hey!" I protest, giving her an offended look. "It would be a shame to squander my natural talents."

"Yep, she kicks ass at beer pong," Jamie chimes in. "Any drinking game, actually. She's awesome at flip cup, too." He continues to stare at me through the fire.

I feel Lucas stiffen beside me. My pulse speeds up and I silently plead for the convo to steer away from my drinking-game prowess.

No such luck. Jamie continues his trip down memory lane. "Remember that tournament after winter formal? You were still in your dress until four a.m. taking on anyone that would agree to play. I think we beat the whole basketball team that night." He chuckles to himself.

I offer him a small smile, hoping that appeases him

enough to stop reminiscing aloud about our past late nights. I see Lucas's jaw clenching out of the corner of my eye.

"I don't even know how you got so good at drinking games," Jake chimes in. "You went to like three parties in high school."

"Yeah, thanks to you," Ash says, jabbing him in the ribs.

He rolls his eyes at her.

"And it's not like we taught you how to play any of them," adds Alex, laughing.

I shrug a shoulder at him. "What can I say? I am gifted in odd ways. And anyway, what you *did* teach me, thank you very much, is how to drive. And I'm not exactly a pro at that, so maybe I should be the one teaching you things from now on." I shoot him a smirk.

"I'm definitely down for some drinking games this weekend," Jamie presses on. "In fact, why don't we head back to the house and get a flip-cup game started right now?"

"I'm up for that," Thomas says excitedly as he stands up from his chair.

"Oooh." Lucy claps her hands and jumps up too. "This will be fun!"

As the rest of the group gets ready to go, Lucas doesn't make a move to get up.

I nudge him with my elbow. "Come on, stick with me, kid. We'll show them how it's done." I wink at him, trying to coax out a laugh. He rolls his eyes at me instead, but I still take it as a victory. He stands up and brushes the sand off his pants. "Let me get that for you," I say with a flirty smile as I start lightly swatting his ass. That gets me the laugh I want, and he puts his arm around me as we follow the crowd back to the house.

≈

Ashley lays down the law as we all wait expectantly, ready to go with our cups filled a quarter way on the table in front of us. "Okay, here are the rules: you have to chug *all* the beer in your cup. *All of it.* Then you put it down and flip the cup over. As soon as it lands flat upside down, the next person goes. No going before the cup lands, and no flipping the cup with any beer in it!"

We're lined up on either side of a long rectangular folding table outside on the patio. Jake, Ash, Thomas, Lucy and Billy on one side, Jamie, Me, Lucas, Alex, Morgan and Greg on the other. Jake agreed to go twice—first and last, to make the teams even. I laugh at this because, from what I remember, he's not exactly a pro at flip cup, but I keep my mouth shut because I'm not about to do the opposing team any favors.

"Ready, go!" Ash shouts, and Jake and Jamie reach out to grab their cups. Jamie swallows all of his beer in one gulp—very impressive; not even a dribble on his chin. Jake takes a bit longer to get his down and some splashes on his t-shirt.

"Come on, come on. Let's go!" We're all cheering them on, everyone shouting at their respective teammate. Jake's first flip is a miss, but Jamie flips his cup over in one shot, and I quickly grab mine and chug it down. Adrenaline pumping through my veins, I set the cup down and flip it over. It lands upside down flat.

"Yes!" Jamie and I shout in unison, and I throw my

hands up, triumphant. He lifts one of his own for a high five, which I meet, beaming with pride.

"Go, go!" I yell to Lucas, who's chugging his own beer next. He misses his first flip, but gets it on the second. "Yes! Nice job," I shout.

"I'm a bit rusty," he says sheepishly, wiping his mouth with the back of his hand.

I wave it off. "Everyone knows the first round is really a practice round," I say with a shrug, and give his arm a squeeze of encouragement.

It's down to the last cup—Greg and Jake are neck and neck. They both fumble with their flips. Jake's cup falls off the table, but Greg gets his on the second try. Our side of the table jumps up and down, screaming like maniacs. Jamie picks me up and twirls me around. I'm so excited that we won, I don't even think twice about it at first. When he sets me down, I see Lucas glaring at us. Crap, that was probably a stupid move. I chalk it up to being momentarily overcome by victory and choose to ignore the whole thing. I keep whooping with excitement, hoping Lucas will let it go.

Ashley catches my eye and gives me a silent warning. I give her a curt nod indicating message received. "Rematch!" she shouts quickly to keep the game going. God bless her, she's always taking all eyes off me when I need her to. "Okay, second cups. We go first this time!" She points to me and back to herself.

Jake counts us down from three and I chug like my life depends on it, barely taking in air, and flip the cup as quickly as I can with shaking hands. I make it on the first try.

"Go, go, go!" I yell at Lucas with beer dribbling down my chin.

Jamie hands me a napkin and we burst out laughing. "This reminds me so much of college," he says between giggles. "You are truly a force to be reckoned with. I would never bet against you in flip cup."

"I think I get better the more I drink!" I laugh harder, really feeling the buzz now. The idea that I do indeed get better the more drunk I get suddenly seems hilarious.

Our team is in the lead and Jamie is up next with the last cup. He gulps his cup down and then flips it like a pro and bam, we're the winners again!

"*Yes!*" Jamie and I look at each other and clutch hands while screaming in each other's faces.

Lucas stands silent beside us, clenching his fists, while the rest of our team cheers on.

The other team watches us from across the table, defeat on their faces. Jake didn't even get to take his turn; that's how quickly we beat them. Ashley is back to eyeing me. Those two beers are hitting me hard now, and I'm having so much fun, I don't really care at this point. It's just a game of flip cup—can't everyone just chill out?

We all seem tipsy after that last round and the volume out here gets loud. Thomas rips off his shirt, picks up Lucy and tosses her in the pool. She screams and splashes him when she surfaces. Morgan and Greg follow suit, jumping fully clothed in after them.

Jamie looks at me, and I instantly know what he's thinking. I shake my head and back away with my hands out. He nods his head, laughing. "Oh yes, you're going in too!" He picks me up and jumps off the edge of the pool with me in his arms.

I come up to the surface blubbering, with my hair in my face, but I can't stop laughing. I swim to the edge of the pool and grab on so I can catch my breath, and look up to see Lucas staring down at me with murder in his eyes.

I ignore his death glare and try to get him to join in on the fun. "Lucas, get in the pool!" He looks unamused with his arms crossed over his chest. "Oh come on, don't be such a party pooper," I say and swim to the stairs. At this point everyone is in the pool except him.

I grab a towel off a lounge chair and wrap it around me. "What's your problem? Come swim with me!" I try to pull his arm, but it's like tugging on a statue. I give him my best flirty smile. "Please?" I bat my wet eyelashes at him a few times for good measure.

After a few seconds he gives in and takes a step forward. In one fell swoop he reaches behind him and pulls the shirt over his head, then grabs my waist and pulls me into the pool with the towel still wrapped around me. We crash into the water, and he doesn't let go, the now soaking-wet towel threatening to drag me down. He quickly finds his footing on the bottom of the pool and lifts me up in his arms out of the water so I can catch my breath.

Grinning, I wrap my arms around his neck and suck in a few lungfuls of air. "See, that wasn't so bad, was it?" I say to him and I lay back against the water and float, his arms keeping me steady, my hair fanning out around me.

Between the beers and the cool water and the feel of Lucas's body next to mine, I'm buzzing with happiness in this moment. The group whoops and hollers while they play around in the pool. Jake is back to throwing Ashley around. Alex does cannonballs off the side. Morgan sits on Greg's shoulders, splashing Billy. It isn't until I catch movement out of the corner of my eye that I'm pulled back to reality.

Jamie gets out of the pool, grabs a towel and stalks inside.

My high quickly deflates as I realize this has the potential to become a real problem, and I'm not sure what to do about it.

CHAPTER 13

I awake to light knocking on the door and my name being whispered in the darkness. "Lila?" I open my eyes and orient myself to the room. The bedside clock says 7:43 a.m. Ugh, who's knocking so early? My head is pounding for the second day in a row.

Lucas peeks his head in. "Lila, are you up?"

"Now I am," I whisper, sitting up, trying not to wake up Ash sleeping next to me. I wonder when she finally came in last night. I was alone when I went to bed around one.

A little while after he threw me in the pool, Lucas reminded me of our plans in the morning and suggested we get some sleep. I didn't expect our plans to start this early. I inwardly cringe as I remember how, in my inebriated state, I may have tried to convince him to come sleep in my bed. He reminded me that Jake and Alex were sleeping on the other side of the wall, so I guess his more sober head prevailed. Good thing, too—I'm not sure I could handle back-to-back walks of shame. Especially in front of my brother.

"Come on, come for a run with me," Lucas says, opening the door wider.

"You didn't say anything about running! What is with everyone and this running?" I hiss at him as I rub my eyes.

He tiptoes in and kneels next to the bed. "Please?" he begs, giving me puppy dog eyes.

FML. So unfair, how can I resist this face?

"Fine," I relent with a sigh. "Just give me a sec to get dressed. And fair warning, it will be more of a power walk for you." I smirk at him. Running is not my thing.

"No problem." He smiles back and tugs a strand of my hair, which I'm sure looks like a disaster right now.

He leaves me to change, and I throw on some workout clothes—a mix of Ash's and mine, I'm sure. I just grabbed whatever I could without turning on the light.

I make my way upstairs into the kitchen, hoping to grab a cup of coffee before the impending doom of exercise. It's empty of people and a complete disaster, beer bottles everywhere—a sure sign that the party kept going long after our departure. No such luck on the coffee, and I decide against picking through the mess to find a coffee pot.

I see Lucas stretching on the patio, and slide open the glass doors to join him outside. He's shirtless, in a pair of running shorts and looking very hot. He grins when he sees me ogling him and points to a cup of coffee sitting on the table. My heart melts when I realize he must have run out earlier just to get this for me.

"Oh my God, you're the best," I say dramatically, and he laughs. I love how thoughtful he is. I grab it gratefully and close my eyes as I inhale the aroma and take a sip. Ah, caffeine. I feel the sun on my face as it rises higher in the sky and open my eyes to see the beautiful early morning glow around us. Maybe I can power through this workout after all.

We jog the two-and-a-half miles to the yacht club in companionable silence, him leading (obviously). He knows I'm not a big runner, and I can tell he's significantly slowing his pace to match mine. I distract myself from the burning in my lungs with the spectacular view of Lucas's back: the way his muscles contract under his skin, the beads of sweat pooling between his shoulder blades. I offer a silent prayer of gratitude for this moment —and for the fact he chose to run shirtless.

We reach the main building and walk around the side to the small beach, which is empty; I guess all the guests are sleeping in. There's a rack of paddleboards on the sand and a little hut next to it where they keep other equipment. Lucas checks the door to see if it's locked. It's not.

He raises a brow at me, eye twinkling with mischief. "Up for a paddle?"

"No way," I say, shaking my head. "What if we get in trouble?"

He chuckles and leans over to kiss my nose. "Live a little."

I tentatively reach out as he hands me a lifejacket from the hut and look around to make sure we're still alone. Lucas pulls a lifejacket on himself, and my face must register disappointment at him covering up his naked torso. He catches my look and smirks at me, causing heat to flood my cheeks.

He slips off his shoes and socks and motions for me to do the same. I hand him my sneakers, and he tucks both our pairs underneath a bush. He carries two boards down the sand and lays them on the water. He reaches out and steadies my board as he holds out a hand to help me onto it.

I hesitate for a beat. I've paddleboarded many times and have excellent balance thanks to years of yoga, so I'm confident I can hold my own. But we're technically stealing these boards, plus being this close to Lucas is unnerving. I'm a little shaky as I accept his hand and climb on.

Once I'm situated, he effortlessly hops on his own board and starts paddling out into the bay. The water is like glass. The sun is higher now and it's glittering over the water. The bright blue sky stretches above us, not a cloud to be seen. We paddle farther out into the channel, and I can see across the water into the backyards of the houses on the other side of the island.

I pause for a beat to soak in the scene around me. "Wow," I say, in awe of how beautiful and peaceful it is out here.

Lucas glides up next to me. "Amazing, right?"

I meet his gaze, smiling. "It's perfect," I say. "Thank you for forcing me out on this thing." I grin at him.

He beams back at me. "Let's keep going," he says, and continues on, his board skimming across the water.

We paddle around the perimeter of the bay, pointing out large houses and admiring their private beaches. One backyard has a big white tent with chairs being arranged for what looks like a wedding right on the lawn. I stop paddling and watch the workers set up, imagining how stunning the wedding will be, right here on the water in this setting.

Lucas notices I've stopped and circles back to me. "Everything okay?" He follows my line of sight to the tent and whistles. "Pretty sweet setup for a wedding."

I nod. "It's always been my dream to get married on the water in Montauk," I admit longingly. "I've always pictured it overlooking the ocean, right at sunset. Maybe rent a house on the bluffs with the waves crashing below."

"Sounds beautiful." He reaches out and squeezes my hand, and I snap back to reality, blushing. If he notices my embarrassment, he doesn't let on.

We start paddling again, and before I know it forty-five minutes have passed. I'm feeling a little crispy; I didn't put on any sunscreen before we left the house. Lucas's shoulders are also looking pink. I tell him so, and suggest we head in.

We paddle back to the beach, which is now busy with little kids playing in the shallow water and their parents lounging on chairs behind them. The lifeguard on duty glares at us from his perch next to the hut, and I give him a sheepish smile as we jump off the boards and drag them back up the sand. We both quickly take off our life vests and put them on the counter of the hut next to him.

"You can't just take the boards without signing them out!" he barks at us.

I mumble an apology as Lucas grabs our shoes, then takes my hand, and we run up to the parking lot, giggling. "I told you we'd get in trouble," I say, trying to catch my breath as he wraps his arms around me and pulls me into his chest.

"Totally worth it," he leans down to whisper in my ear, tightening his grip around my body. He plants a kiss on my neck. "Your skin is so hot," he says, smiling against it.

"I know, I'm so burnt!" I squeal as he traces kisses across my collarbone. I lean my head back as he trails up my jawline.

"You are so sexy," he whispers, and leans his forehead against mine. "That was fun. See, aren't you glad you got out of bed?"

"Yes, definitely," I agree, closing my eyes as his lips touch mine.

My phone chirps in my pocket, and Lucas groans.

"Back to reality," I say with a grin as I fish it out. Ashley's name is flashing on the screen. "Hi Ash, what's up?"

"Where the hell did you disappear to so early?" she asks on the other end.

"Lucas and I ran to the yacht club and stole paddleboards," I answer like it's a typical morning for me.

"What? Who is this? Where's Lila?"

I laugh at her response. "I know, I guess I'm a rebel now. I blame it on the bad influence in front of me." I quirk a brow at him, and he cracks a smile as he watches me talk on the phone.

"Well whenever he's done corrupting you, come meet us at the beach," she says, and hangs up.

I put the phone back in my pocket and grin at him. "Looks like we're heading to the beach."

I have some trouble getting Lucas out of the house when we stop home to change into our bathing suits, as he has other ideas when he sees me in my bikini. I finally convince him our friends will definitely know what we're up to if we take any longer, and we walk the few blocks over to the beach.

Our group is easy to spot—a spread-out semi-circle of

beach chairs facing the ocean, a big cooler in the center and two surfboards lying on the sand to the side.

Ash jumps up from her seat next to Jake and runs over. "Finally! I've been waiting all day for you guys," she exclaims, grabbing my arm.

"See," I mouth at Lucas, and he gives me a mischievous grin in return.

Ashley drags me to the open chair next to her and pulls me down to sit. "Where'd you go? Did you have fun? Tell me everything."

I laugh at her machine-gun questioning and look around us at all the empty chairs. "Where is everyone?" I ask. Only Jake and Ashley are here.

"Oh, Alex saw some girls he knows down there somewhere." She gestures down the beach in the other direction. "Thomas, Billy, Morgan and Greg went to the Ditch Witch to get food, and Jamie and Lucy are surfing. Look, there they are." She points them out to me in the water.

I spot them sitting on their boards in the sea of other surfers. I quickly glance at Lucas and see he's engaged in conversation with my brother. I lean closer to Ash. "How was Jamie this morning?" I whisper.

She shrugs. "He seemed totally fine. Jake and I went to the bakery to get breakfast, and when we got back everyone was already in the backyard around the pool."

I blow out a sigh of relief. "Good. He kind of left in a huff last night," I say, biting my cheek.

"Lila's involved in a love triangle!" She teases me.

I roll my eyes at her. "But really, who'd have thought, right?" I ask, shaking my head at the ridiculousness of it.

She nudges me with her arm. "When are you gonna realize how hot you are? Speaking of, take off your cover-

137

up. Let's see who else we can reel in with that hot little body of yours." She tugs at the hem of my dress.

I scoff at her but oblige and pull it over my head. "You mean *your* cover-up."

"What's mine is yours, babe." She winks at me with a grin. "But all jokes aside, did you tell Lucas about Jamie yet?" she asks, her face serious now.

I let out a groan under my breath. "No," I say hesitantly, and now she gives me an eye roll. "I know, I know, I just didn't want to ruin the moment. It's never a good time. But I will...eventually," I say, knowing I have to be honest. I want to be honest. We're just having so much fun and I'm scared that the idea of my ex-boyfriend staying in the same house with us all weekend will spook Lucas.

My eyes trace back to Jamie and Lucy in the water with the other surfers. He always said he was happiest on his surfboard. Lucy looks pretty happy, too. She's really good at this; I watch her effortlessly catch a wave without so much as a wobble. Jamie follows suit just as smoothly. He barely paddles to catch the wave, pops up gracefully and rides it all the way to shore. They both make it look so easy. I wish I could surf. Jamie always promised he would teach me how to one day, and I feel a pang of disappointment that we never got around to it.

I watch as he picks up his board and walks out of the water to where Lucy is waiting for him, holding hers on the sand. As they make their way over to us, I study his face, trying to read his mood. He looks happy and exhilarated from being out in the ocean.

"Oh hey, you're here," he says when he spots me and comes over to my chair, setting his board down on the sand next to me. Lucy puts hers next to his and starts wringing out her hair.

"Yup, hi. Here I am," I say. "You guys look good out there." I gesture to the water.

"Thanks," he says with a smile and sits down next to me.

I quickly glance at Lucas, who's still chatting with Jake.

"The water is great." Lucy unzips her wetsuit so it hangs at her waist. "You guys should come in."

"Yeah, how about that surf lesson I've always promised you?" Jamie says, and I look at him, startled, wondering briefly if he can read my mind.

I hesitate. Lucas and I just had such a great morning, I don't want to ruin it by surfing with Jamie. But on the other hand, I really have always wanted to learn how. Plus, it won't be just the two of us out there. My eyes track back to the many other surfers who are already in the water.

Luckily, I don't even have to answer because Ashley hops out of her chair and yells, "Yes! Let's learn to surf!" before I can even say anything.

Jake and Lucas pause their conversation and look over at her bouncing up and down in front of me on the sand.

"This will be so great. I've always wanted to learn to surf—and so have you, Li!" She reaches down for my hands to pull me up from my chair.

Lucy laughs at Ash's excitement and unzips the rest of her wetsuit so she can peel it off. She steps out of it revealing her pink, striped one-piece underneath, and hands it to Ash. "Sure, let's do it. The waves are the perfect size to learn. Put that on," she instructs her. "And we can just borrow Thomas and Billy's boards," she adds, pointing to the two abandoned boards lying in the sand next to us.

Jamie studies my face, waiting for my answer, not seeming to register Ash and Lucy's enthusiasm.

I let Ash pull me up and look over at Lucas's reaction. I give him a small shrug of my shoulder, silently asking if he thinks this is a good idea. He smiles in return, which I take as a yes. I turn back to Jamie, who seems annoyed to have just witnessed our wordless exchange. The tightness in his eyes is back, but he gets up, brushes the sand off his suit and says, "Guess we're going surfing."

I help Ash wrestle herself into Lucy's wetsuit.

"I wish I had an extra, Lila. But I only brought this one with me," Lucy says apologetically.

"I'll give you mine," Jamie says, and starts unzipping his.

"No, no, it's okay. I don't need one," I say, holding out my hand to stop him.

He pauses and looks at me, his brows furrowed. "You hate being cold," he states plainly.

This is true, I do hate being cold. And wet. Maybe this isn't a good idea after all, I think, my shoulders tensing up.

He reads the uncertainty on my face and realizes I'm about to change my mind. "Thomas has a rash guard!" he blurts out, running over to grab it from where it's draped over the empty chair.

"Oh, good call, J," Lucy pipes in. "That's perfect for you, Lila. Your legs might be cold but you'll get used to it. I don't even feel the water anymore," she says, assuring Ash she doesn't need a wetsuit.

I blow out a breath. Now that that's settled, I can't really back out, can I?

Lucy and Jamie get on their boards right there in the sand and show us the basics of how to paddle out and pop up once you catch the wave. They make us do a few practice pop-ups until we feel comfortable with the movement and confident we can nail it. However, that confidence wanes when I realize it's probably very different in the water, especially when waves are crashing on you. After we assure them we're ready, we each pick up a board and it's go-time.

Jake and Lucas follow us down to the water. Lucas can sense my trepidation. "You don't have to do this if you don't want to," he says to me.

"She's always wanted to learn how to surf," Jamie says defensively, narrowing his eyes at Lucas.

"No, I want to, just a bit nervous is all. It's a little different from paddleboarding," I say, thinking about the peacefulness I felt this morning, gliding through the bay with Lucas by my side. I offer him a small smile to assure him I'm okay.

"Once you get the hang of it, it'll be easy," Lucy pipes in. "And like I said, the waves aren't very big today," she adds with an encouraging grin.

"I'm more concerned about this one. You may be a runner, but balance isn't your strong suit," Jake teases Ashley as he pokes her side. She squeals and drops her board on the sand to splash him. He picks her up and tosses her over his shoulder and wades deeper into the water as she giggles louder.

While they've captured everyone else's attention, Lucas turns to me. "You're gonna do great," he says and squeezes my hand.

I return the gesture with a smile and place the board

in the water. "Thanks. I'll see you in a bit," I say to him and wade out to where Jamie is waiting.

Lucas and Jake watch from the shore as we paddle out of the shallows. Jamie and Lucy guide us through the incoming waves, giving us tips on how not to get clobbered as they crash on top of us. We finally make our way to the lineup, where other surfers are bobbing on their boards waiting for that perfect wave. Jamie sits up on his board and points out the other surfers' movements as they position themselves in front of the wave and start paddling to catch it. Lucy is doing the same thing with Ash a few feet away. After studying up-close how they wait for the right time to start paddling, and the exact moment to pop up when you feel the wave lift you, Ash and I are ready to give it a try.

"Okay, here comes your wave. I'm gonna push you to start and you have to keep paddling until I say get up," Jamie says as a wave approaches us.

I position myself on the board and get ready to paddle. My heart hammers in my ears in anticipation.

"Go, go, go!" yells Jamie, and I start to paddle like my life depends on it. I feel a surge as he pushes the back of my board to catch the incoming wave.

"Now! Pop up now, Lila!" he yells, and I push myself up on the board just like he showed us on the sand. I feel shaky as I try to get my balance, but I manage to stay up for about five seconds before a little kid on his own board heads straight toward me and I tumble over. Panic floods through me as I crash into the water, and the leash from the board pulls my leg down as I try to kick to the surface. My other foot finds the sea floor and I am able to shoot myself up, gulping down huge lungfuls of air as I finally break free. I look around to orient myself and start to laugh when I realize I'm in shallow water.

I look over to where Jamie is paddling frantically to me. "Are you okay?" he says, voice panicked, jumping off his board as he reaches me, his eyes wide with alarm. "You got up great, but I saw that kid heading straight for you and then boom, you went down." His frown eases when he realizes I'm laughing.

"That little fucker startled me and I lost my balance," I say, wiping water from my eyes.

He runs a hand through his hair. "Don't worry, I think I scared the shit out of him," he says with a guilty look. "His older sister looked at me like I was crazy for cursing out a pre-teen." He sees my shocked expression and starts to laugh at himself.

"Let's go again!" I say and get back on the board, eager to give it another try.

His brows raise. "Seriously? You're ready to go again?" I guess my wipeout looked pretty bad.

"Of course. Did that look like surfing to you? I'm determined to learn how to surf!" I say over my shoulder, already paddling back out.

"Okay then," he says and gives me a push back in the direction we started before following on his own board.

Just then, I see Ashley get up on a wave. She screams with her arms in the air, but quickly loses her balance and nose-dives into the water, just like I did two minutes ago.

Jamie and I burst out laughing.

"Is that what I looked like?" I ask him, face hot with embarrassment.

"Not quite. You were much more graceful," he reassures me.

"Liar!" I splash him in the face, and he looks at me with mock horror as we both continue to paddle.

We rejoin Lucy, who also seems to be amused by Ashley. "Well, at least you both made it up for a hot minute," she says to me with a grin.

"I'm going again," I say, determined to actually stay up this time.

And I do. It starts out the same—with Jamie pushing me into the wave—and I paddle as hard as I can until I hear him scream, "Now, Lila, now!"

I push myself up, and this time I remember not to look down as I swing my leg under me and bend my knees deep, and just like that I'm surfing.

"I'm *surfing*!" I yell to nobody in particular, in awe of myself as I glide through the water. This time no kid cuts me off, nobody gets in my way, and I ride the wave in.

I see Jake and Lucas yelling and waving from down the beach where they're watching us. I wave back at them, and quickly look behind me to see Jamie, Lucy and Ash also cheering me on from their perch in the lineup. I remember how Jamie told me to just straddle the board and sit down when I want to stop instead of jumping off into the water, so that's what I attempt to do. Somehow I manage to execute a more graceful dismount than before, and once I'm down I can't hide my grin as I think how much fun that was—so much more exhilarating than paddleboarding. I am instantly hooked. All I can think about is that I need to do it again, so I turn around and paddle back out.

"That was awesome!" Jamie exclaims as I approach them, reaching out to high five me over his board.

"That felt truly amazing. I think I get it now," I say, grinning like crazy.

"You're a natural, Lila," says Lucy.

I can't stop smiling. "Doesn't hurt that these are baby waves today," I say, grateful the ocean decided to go easy on me my first time out. I've seen the surf at this beach get pretty wild, so I know it's not always such favorable conditions.

They both nod in agreement.

"Okay, I'm gonna attempt that," Ash says, pointing at me.

We laugh, but encourage her to give it another try.

This time she's up for about two seconds longer than before, but nose-dives again. I go a third time and catch another wave just like before, riding it all the way to shore, screaming my head off. And it goes like that for a while, us taking turns, Ash and I catching some waves, and wiping out on some too. Lucy and Jamie rotate in a few times while Ash and I cheer them on.

After a while Ashley's lips are blue, and she says she's calling it a day. Lucy also says she's cold and tired and wants to head in. I'm not ready to go in just yet, and Jamie agrees to stay out for a little while longer with me. I lose track of time in the water, studying the other surfers and enjoying the rush of adrenaline as I go for each wave. Some time later, Jamie tells me that it's 4 p.m. already and doesn't see our group on the beach anymore.

"Oh no, is it really that late?" I say, completely surprised at how long we've been out here for. I look to where our setup was, and he's right—I don't see our circle of chairs anymore, or our friends anywhere. Yikes, I wonder how long ago they decided to leave. I've been so absorbed by surfing, I didn't notice them packing up.

"Okay, let's ride this one in," I say, and look behind me to see a wave approaching. I ride it to shallow water

145

where I can start to see to the bottom and get distracted when I see a crab on the ocean floor. I lean over a little too far on the board, lose my balance and crash into the water. My knee knocks into a rock and pain radiates down my leg. I cry out and hobble up to the surface, trying to catch my balance and grab the board from getting sucked back into the current.

Jamie sees me struggling and jumps into the water, making his way over through the crashing surf. I manage to drag my board to the sand and collapse on top, blood dripping down my leg.

"Oh shit, Lila, are you okay?" He tosses his board on the sand next to mine and squats down to assess the damage, his face pinched with concern as he studies the gash on my knee.

"Ow," I yelp as he reaches out to touch my leg. "It stings like crazy," I say, wincing.

"Do you think you can walk on it?"

I stand up and test my weight on it. It doesn't hurt so much. "Yeah, I can walk. I think it actually looks worse than it is," I sigh out with relief. "It's more the cut that's burning from the salt water."

"Okay, good." He nods at me. "Let's head back to the house and get it cleaned up. We need to rinse it out so it doesn't get infected."

I limp behind him up the beach to where the group was sitting and I see my beach bag and two towels left in the sand. Jamie grabs one of the towels and wipes the blood off my leg. Thankfully the stinging is subsiding a bit, but the cut is still bleeding. I grab the bag and he heaves a surfboard under each arm and starts walking up to the parking lot.

"Wait, I can carry one. I'm not seriously injured!" I protest, following behind him.

He scoffs. "Please, these are lightweight, I got them. Just worry about hobbling your way back to the house," he says with a smirk.

"I'm not hobbling," I mutter under my breath and make a face, but follow him anyway, secretly grateful I don't have to schlep a board home myself.

Fortunately the house is only a few blocks away, and I make it there just fine. Jamie places the boards in the rack outside the garage and we make our way around the back of the house. Lucas, Jake and Alex are sitting around the table, deep in conversation, and look startled when they see us walk into the yard. All three pairs of eyes zero in on the blood rushing down my leg and they immediately jump up from their chairs.

Lucas is out of his seat and across the yard next to me before I can even blink. "Are you okay? What the hell happened?" he bellows, glaring at Jamie like it's somehow his fault.

"I'm fine, Lucas. I just knocked my knee on a rock. It looks worse than it is," I say gently, trying to calm him down.

Alex and Jake watch with concern as we cross the yard.

"She's okay. She's a trooper," Jamie says to them all, ignoring Lucas.

"A 'trooper'? She's leaving a trail of fucking blood behind her," Lucas shouts at him, eyes bulging out of his head.

Alex pulls his chair out for me to sit, and as Lucas helps me in it, Jake sets another one in front of me to put my leg on. "That looks pretty bad, Li. Are you sure you're okay?" my brother asks, eyes tight with worry. He attempts to reach out and wipe the blood with a napkin, then decides against it and pulls his hand back, cringing.

"Yes, yes, really, I'm fine. I swear," I assure them all as four pairs of eyes study me critically.

"Why don't you make yourself useful and get her some ice," Lucas snaps at Jamie.

"Lucas!" I yell at him.

Jamie clenches his jaw but looks at me. "It's okay, Lila. Ice is a good idea. I'll be right back." He walks inside the house.

I turn to face Lucas. "What is wrong with you?" I hiss at him. "You don't have to be so rude."

"What is wrong with *me*?" he hisses back. "You were out there with this guy in the water all day, totally ignored us when we tried to tell you we were leaving, and then he brings you home limping with your leg a bloody, mangled mess." His voice raises an octave with every word.

I look at Alex and Jake for help, and get none as they look away, avoiding my eyes. I take a deep breath and try to keep my voice calm. "First of all, I totally lost track of time and I did *not* ignore you. I didn't even see you guys leave. Second, this is just a scratch. I told you, it looks a lot worse than it is." I lean over to look at the wound and wince at the blood still oozing from it.

Jamie comes back out with ice and a first aid kit. "I found this in the bathroom." He waves the kit in his hand.

Lucas snatches it from him. "I'll take it from here."

"Dude, chill, okay?" Jamie glares at him. I can tell he's trying hard not to lose his temper, but he looks awfully close to his breaking point. Lucas is kind of being a dick right now.

"Lucas, stop being so rude." I grab the first aid kit

from him. "Jamie, it's okay. You can go shower if you want, I got this. Really, I'm fine, I promise. Thank you for helping me back." I offer him an encouraging smile.

He studies my face, unsure of what to do. He looks to Jake and Alex, then back at me, sizing up the situation. I can tell he doesn't want to leave me, but he also doesn't want a fight right now, and three against one isn't exactly fair. "Okay Lila, if you're sure."

"She's sure." Lucas continues to scowl at him.

Jamie shakes his head with an eye roll and turns around and walks inside.

"That was incredibly uncalled for, Lucas," I say pointedly.

The moment stretches as we wordlessly stare daggers at each other.

Alex gently takes the first aid kit out of my hand and opens it, takes out an alcohol swab, rips it open with his teeth and starts to dab around the cut.

"Ow!" I hiss, breaking eye contact with Lucas as the alcohol stings my leg.

"Sorry, sorry," Alex says, blowing on my knee. "Have to make sure it's not infected. Do you know how much bacteria the ocean carries?"

"Not helping, dude," Jake whispers to him.

Alex shrugs. "It's true though," he mutters to himself, squirting some antibacterial ointment onto the cut.

I grit my teeth and sigh. After the stinging subsides, I glance at each of their faces. "I'm sorry, I really didn't see you guys calling out to me, I swear. I wouldn't ignore you on purpose," I say to them, but mostly to Lucas.

He scrubs a hand down his face and lets out a long breath. He turns his attention to my leg. "Alex, it's not bad?"

"Nope, good as new," Alex says as he places two Band-Aids in an *X* on top of my knee.

Lucas nods. "Okay, thanks. Do you guys mind if I have a minute with Lila, then?"

"Sure, we were about to go change anyway. We're supposed to be leaving for dinner in less than an hour," my brother says, looking at his watch.

Alex looks at me with a furrowed brow, silently assessing if I'm truly okay.

I give him a smile and a wink. "Thanks, Doc, I appreciate it."

He nods, apparently satisfied, and follows my brother inside.

I turn to Lucas and grab his hand. "Hey, I really am sorry," I say softly, squeezing his hand.

He presses his lips together, looking back at me, and I can see the hurt in his eyes. "You were out there with him all afternoon. I didn't know what to think," he finally says, pulling his gaze from mine.

"I really lost track of time. And I didn't see you calling to me; I was so absorbed in surfing, really. It had nothing to do with him." I squeeze his hand again, trying to get him to look at me. "Lucas, there's nothing going on between me and Jamie. It was just surfing. Promise," I say with emphasis, and tug his arm down so he stoops to my level. I reach out and grab a fistful of his shirt and pull him in for a kiss. "You're the only one I want," I say against his lips.

He lets out a sigh and I feel his shoulders relax. "Glad to hear." He kisses me lightly, then rests his forehead against mine.

"Really, I'm sorry. I don't want to fight," I say.

He looks at me with concern. "Are you sure your knee is okay?"

I hop up from my chair and do a little dance to prove I'm not seriously injured. "See? Good as new."

His expression brightens. "This feels a lot like when you catapulted out of that tree when we were kids. Except the roles are reversed."

I bark out a laugh as the memory forms in my mind. "I really thought I killed you that day! Should we go in and get ready for dinner?"

He puts his arm around my shoulders and leads me inside, and I sigh out in relief that all is well. For now.

CHAPTER 14

We have dinner at Topside restaurant at Gosman's Dock, looking out over the water at the boats passing through the inlet below. Jamie keeps his distance and sits at the opposite end of the table, taking a breather from Lucas. Lucas finally relaxes, and is over the drama from earlier and seems to be having a good time. Jake and Ashley continue their canoodling throughout dinner, while Alex and I give each other looks across the table. I still haven't gotten a chance to discuss this budding romance with Ash since we haven't had a moment alone, but I actually think they're kind of cute together. After the initial shock, the idea is growing on me. Who better for my brother than my best friend?

After the check is paid, we decide to go to a bar in town called The Point. Being the Fourth of July weekend, town is crazy busy and the line to get into the bar is wrapped around the block. Billy, Greg and Morgan decide to head back to the house, not wanting to wait in line. When the rest of us finally get in, the bar is mobbed with people.

Ash, Lucy and I somehow find an empty corner near the bar and set up shop while the guys fight for the bartender's attention.

"You were awesome out there in the water today, Lila," Lucy says to me with a proud smile. "Such a natural."

"Thanks, I loved it so much." I immediately remember how amazing it felt gliding on top of the water. "I've been wanting to learn how to surf for so long."

"Think you'll get back out there tomorrow?" she asks.

I hesitate and look at Ash for a beat, recalling the earful she gave me when we were getting ready about ditching Lucas all afternoon. As much as I would love to surf again, I don't think a repeat with Jamie is the best idea, and I can tell she feels the same by the expression on her face right now. My spirits plummet as I realize my surfing career is probably going to be extremely short-lived. "Probably not the best idea with this knee," I say. "What are the plans for tomorrow, anyway?" I ask, changing the subject.

"Beach during the day and probably just have another bonfire at night. Maybe stop by that pool party? Town is just way too crazy to try to go out anywhere this weekend," Lucy says, gesturing around the crowded bar to emphasize her point. "There is usually a big beach party every Fourth, so it should be a good time."

The guys squeeze through the crowd and hand us our drinks.

"This place is a madhouse," my brother complains. He reaches up to wipe the perspiration from his forehead and frowns.

"It's Fourth of July weekend, what do you expect?" Alex shrugs a shoulder at him.

A group gets up from a high top behind us and Lucy runs over and grabs it before anyone else can. "Thank God!" Ash says as she claims a chair and puts her bag on the table.

Lucas and Thomas see their friends from the beer store across the bar and go over to say hello. A Rihanna song that Ashley loves comes blaring out of the speakers and she screams and grabs Jake's hand, pulling him onto the dance floor with her. He rolls his eyes but follows her with a goofy grin on his face. Alex laughs at them and looks back at me, brows wiggling. He tugs me from my chair to follow them.

I groan and try to object, blaming my knee, but he rolls his eyes at me. "Your knee is fine, and you know it!"

I relent and let him pull me onto the dance floor. "What is going on with them?" I lean in to ask him over the music, nodding my chin at Jake and Ash dancing next to us.

He shrugs, grinning. "Why? Does it bother you?" he asks me, cocking his head.

"No," I answer, but wrinkle my nose in distaste. "It's just...weird."

He gives me a patronizing look. "Hey now, I thought we established that we're all adults here."

"I know, I know. I'm just saying, for the record, Jake definitely cannot give me any shit now," I mutter to him.

"Believe me, I don't think he cares anymore." He laughs as he watches my brother and my best friend grinding on the dance floor.

I make a puke face at him, then crack a smile myself. If they make each other this happy, I'm glad for them.

We dance for a few songs until we're all sweaty and the guys decide to take a breather and get us another round of drinks. Between the two glasses of wine at dinner and the beer I just drank too fast, I should probably slow down, but I'm having too much fun. I can barely feel any pain in my knee, and the DJ is on a roll with his set. Ash and I stay out on the dance floor, dancing in our own little space, when all of a sudden I feel someone knock into me.

"Oh, I'm sorry, Miss," says Jamie in mock apology, a hand covering his mouth. He takes my hand and twirls me a few times, then does this ridiculous dance move that he always used to do in college. I crack up like I always have when I witness it. It's basically a combo of the cabbage patch, the running man and the sprinkler, and he looks absolutely insane doing it. Lucy and Ash start laughing too, then we all attempt to copy him. A few people next to us catch on, and pretty soon everyone on the dance floor is doing this silly routine. I have to stop and catch my breath, I'm laughing so hard.

"Well that caught on quick," he leans in and says to me proudly, eyes shining. A new song comes on and he takes my hand and starts twirling me around again, both of us still giggling. When the song ends, I take a beat to wipe the sweat from my brow and realize the guys never came back with our drinks. I look over at our table and see Jake and Alex watching us with sour looks on their faces.

I leave Jamie with the girls on the dance floor and go back to the table. "What's with the death glares? And what happened to my drink?" I ask, annoyed as I realize how thirsty I am. I reach out and grab Alex's beer and take a long gulp.

"Lila, what are you doing?" my brother asks me, a sharp edge to his tone.

I narrow my eyes at him. "Um, dancing? Like

everyone else but you two party poopers." I hand the beer back to Alex and look around for the rest of our group. "Where's Lucas, anyway?"

"He left," Jake says.

My eyes snap back to him. "What? Why?"

Jake points to the dance floor. "He saw you dancing with Jamie. Said he didn't want to cause a scene, but he wasn't staying here to watch you two grinding all night."

"'*Grinding*'? That was hardly grinding! Did you not see practically the whole bar out there dancing? Ash and Lucy are out there, too! *Jesus*, nothing is going on with us!" I grab the beer back out of Alex's hand and take another swig.

I get that Lucas was annoyed with me surfing for so long earlier, but this is just nuts. The whole fucking bar was dancing. I can't believe he would just leave without telling me.

Jake and Alex look at each other, conducting a wordless communication that I'm not privy to.

"What?" I ask, barely containing my irritation.

The moment stretches, neither of them speaking. I roll my hand at them, gesturing for them to start talking.

"Um, there's something else," my brother says finally, avoiding my gaze.

"What? Spit it out," I say, my words sharp.

"Well..."

"Jake kind of let it slip that you and Jamie dated for a few years," Alex finishes for him.

I feel my eyes pop out of my head. "What?" I gape at my brother as panic runs down my spine.

Jake rubs his neck, looking contrite. "It's not my fault! How was I supposed to know you didn't tell him who Jamie really was?"

"Oh my God." I drop my head into my hands and collapse back onto the empty stool.

"Why would you tell Luke that you two 'just hooked up a few times'?" Alex asks me, his head tilting in confusion.

"I didn't exactly say it like that," I say, looking up at him through my hands.

"Well, according to him you said it precisely like that," Jakes pipes in, judgment lacing his tone.

I sigh, feeling defeated. "I couldn't find the right moment in the last couple of days to tell him that we're sharing a house with my college boyfriend, okay? I was going to come clean eventually, really—I was planning on it. But then we had so much fun this morning, and I didn't want to spoil the day." I narrow my eyes at them. "I didn't think you two would fucking out me!" I point an accusatory finger in their direction.

"I'm sorry!" My brother puts his hands up. "I was actually trying to make it better by saying Luke has nothing to worry about since Jamie is your *ex*-boyfriend for a reason. And when he heard that word he kind of lost it and demanded we tell him exactly how long you two were together for, because *you* just told him that it was barely anything. And then there you are, dry-humping this guy on the dance floor right in front of his face!" He shakes his head, exasperated.

My head rears back and I almost fall off my chair. "We weren't even close to 'dry-humping.' The whole bar was dancing! Jamie grabbed my hand and twirled me a few times. Big fucking deal! I can't control what Jamie does. And for the last fucking time, nothing is going on with us. And it's okay that Lucas just takes off without saying goodbye? Ditching me here without a word?" I am starting to really sweat, and I reach up to gather the hair off my neck with shaking hands.

Alex jumps in to calm us both down. "Okay, okay. Everyone just relax. But honestly, Li, it doesn't really look like nothing, not if you put together everything that's happened over the last two days. Jamie is clearly still into you. Plus, you lied to Lucas about him, which makes you look guilty. Why would you lie if nothing is going on? Looks to me like you need to make a choice here," Alex says, palms open. He gives me an empathetic look to soften the blow of his words.

I'm not having it; I roll my eyes dramatically at him. "There is no choice. Jamie is not an option. We *did* break up for a reason. And I told you, it just wasn't the right time to tell Lucas our history. I didn't get a fucking chance!"

I realize I'm shrieking at them in the middle of this bar and I pause to take a breath and lower my voice. Yelling at each other is not helping the situation. "Look, I know I should've been honest from the start. Lucas just came back into my life after all this time, and I didn't want anything to jeopardize our second chance. Jamie wasn't even supposed to be here this weekend, I was completely thrown by him showing up. I panicked and I didn't know how to handle it, so I just let Lucas believe it was only a casual college fling. But seriously, I swear, I'm only interested in Lucas." I hold each of their gazes for a beat.

"Well maybe you should start acting like it," my brother says. I shoot him a murderous glare, which he shrugs off. "We're just saying, he seemed pretty pissed. And from my point of view, he kind of has a reason to be, especially after you ditched him for so long on your surf lesson with your ex. Before you got home from the beach, he sat us down to have a man-to-man talk about you two. He said he didn't want a repeat of high school, and that he was laying it all out in the open because he wants to give it a serious shot. He made us assure him that we're okay with it before moving forward," he says, his hands splayed out on the table.

I flinch, surprised. Lucas talked to them about his feelings? That definitely doesn't sound like the Lucas I know. I'm impressed, actually—his emotional maturity has come a long way. Which only makes me feel worse about hiding the truth from him.

Alex reads the skepticism on my face and nods to agree with Jake. "It's true, he did, Lila. And he was devastated when he found out that you lied to him about Jamie. You should have seen his face; it was pretty terrible." He winces at the memory.

"Like you kicked his puppy," my brother adds with a frown.

"Not helping," Alex hisses under his breath.

I ignore them as I take a minute to process all of this. The realization that I seriously fucked up here hits me like a ton of bricks. I really didn't mean to lie to Lucas; I guess I was just terrified that something would derail us so soon after finding our way back to each other. I didn't want to ruin what was happening between us. I don't even know what is happening between us. This has all happened so fast. And with him being jealous of Jamie from the start of the weekend, I thought it would only get worse if I told him our history was more serious than he was led to believe.

I messed up big-time—I see that now. By trying to

avoid the drama, I caused so much more than if I'd just been honest from the start.

The guys see this revelation play out on my face. They both look at me with sympathy. "Look, I think you just need to tell him how you feel about him," Alex says softly.

"And maybe stop running off with this dude in front of him," Jake adds with a teasing grin.

Again, I shoot him my best scowl.

"That look will help too," Alex nods in agreement, a faint smile on his lips.

I snort at them. "You guys are morons. But you're right, I need to talk to him. How long ago did he leave?"

"About fifteen minutes," Jake answers, looking at the time on his phone.

Ashley and Lucy come back to the table and sit down. "Where are our drinks? I'm dying." Ashley fans herself with her hands.

"It must be a million degrees in here," Lucy agrees, looking around the crowded bar. "Where is everyone, anyway? Is it time to leave yet?" she adds, spotting Thomas still chatting with his friends in the corner and waving him over.

"I'm ready to leave, how about you guys?" Ash asks the rest of us.

"Fine with me," my brother says, offering her the rest of his beer.

She takes it and finishes it in one gulp.

"I'll go get Jamie." Lucy goes to grab him off the dance floor, where he's now twirling a leggy blonde as her friends laugh and dance nearby.

"See?" I point this out to Alex and Jake. "It's just dancing," I say, my tone sharp.

They both give me an eye roll.

"What's just dancing?" Ashley asks, confused. "What's going on now? Where is Lucas?"

The guys look at me.

"He got mad that I was dancing with Jamie and bailed," I answer, stifling my own eye roll.

It takes her a minute to register my words. "Wait, what? He saw you dancing and left without saying goodbye? Wow." She lets out a long breath and leans back on her stool.

"Not *quite* how it went down..." Jake pipes in, opening a palm in my direction.

"Well, what am I missing then?" She looks at each of us, confusion clouding her expression.

I sigh and explain what happened, feeling even more guilty as I relay all the details.

"Yikes, Lila." She gives me a sympathetic look.

"I know, I know," I say, hunched over in defeat as nausea pools in my stomach. "Alright, let's go so I can fix this." I gesture for everyone to get moving and lead the group out of the bar.

We have to wait thirty minutes just to get an Uber home. The main street in town is packed with people walking in and out of bars and restaurants. Almost every place has a line out the door to get in. There is a group of rowdy teenagers goofing off in the street. My stress level is rising, and I am itching to get home already so I can talk to Lucas. Finally, the Uber comes; it's an old-school station wagon with a third row. It's a tight squeeze for our group. Thomas gets in the front, Alex goes straight to the far back and Ash sits on Jake's lap in the second row with Lucy in the middle and Jamie scooting in beside them.

"Want to sit on my lap, Li?" Jamie asks me, hopeful. His face falls when I say, "I'll just get in the back with Alex," and climb over them.

I settle in next to Alex and he gives my arm a squeeze. I offer him a small smile and turn my head to look out the window, trying to sift through the tornado of thoughts in my head. I need to figure out what the hell I'm going to say to Lucas. If he's as mad as the guys described, I have some serious groveling to do.

The Uber pulls into the driveway and everyone unloads and heads around to the backyard.

Jamie hangs back and waits for me to climb out of the car. "Can we talk for a minute, Lila?" he asks me hesitantly.

I pause and watch as the group disappears around the house, eager to get inside and talk to Lucas. I inwardly sigh. This is the last thing I want to do, but I can't exactly say no. "Sure, what's up?" I ask, trying to smooth out the annoyance in my tone.

He grabs my hand and looks like he's struggling with whatever it is he wants to say. He starts and stops a couple of times before I feel my patience wearing thin.

"What is it, Jamie? Just tell me." I want him to spit it out already so I can go find Lucas.

A look of resolve passes across his face, and he forges forward. "Okay, so I've been thinking about this for a while now. I think we made a mistake. Maybe we should've tried to make it work instead of just breaking up. And I feel like this weekend, us being here together unplanned, is some kind of sign. I've really missed you, Lila. These last couple of days with you have solidified for me just how much I want you in my life. I don't know what's going on with you and that Lucas guy, but I do know how I feel about you. And you can't tell me you don't feel anything too."

He reaches out and grabs my face with both of his hands, pulling me closer to him. I'm so stunned by his words that I don't stop him. I'm so caught off guard that my mind is having trouble processing what's happening right now. He mistakes my silence for encouragement. "I've missed this so much," he whispers right before he touches his lips to mine.

I don't even have a chance to react. One moment he's kissing me and then all of a sudden he's flying backwards across the lawn. I blink, and Lucas has him by the shirt collar, a murderous look in his eyes. My jaw drops and my hand flies to my mouth.

"What the fuck is your problem?" he screams in Jamie's face, right before he winds his arm back and punches him.

"Fuck!" Jamie howls as he falls back, grabbing his nose, blood dripping down his face.

"Holy shit, Lucas!" I shriek at him, unable to believe my eyes.

"Don't 'Lucas' me! You were making out with the guy!" He yells back at me, his chest heaving.

"He just kissed me out of nowhere. I was just about to push him away!" I try to defend myself through the lump forming in my throat.

He takes a breath to calm his shallow breathing and scrubs a hand down his face. "How could I believe that? You've been lying to me about him all weekend, Lila," he accuses me, pointing to Jamie, who's still on the ground pinching his nose with his head held back.

I wince at the truth of his words. "I know," I say, wringing my hands. "I did lie about our history, and I'm truly sorry. I was going to tell you the truth, I swear, but it was never the right moment. We were having such a good time, and I didn't want to spoil the weekend. But I promise you, there's nothing going on now—it's completely over between us!" I say with sincerity, trying to keep the panic from shaking my voice. I take a step toward him, attempting to catch his gaze.

"It didn't look like it from where I was standing," Lucas scoffs, shaking his head and avoiding my eyes. His body vibrates with anger.

"Lila, don't say that. It's not over. I love you," Jamie pleads, crumpled on the grass.

"Jamie, I'm sorry but I don't feel that way about you. I don't think I ever did," I say sadly, my eyes filled with remorse.

"How can you say that?" he protests, still clutching his nose, his voice wobbling. He looks completely crushed, and it breaks my heart.

I slowly shrug my shoulder. "I'm sorry, but it's the truth. And I think deep down you know it too," I say softly.

"This is bullshit," he sputters and gets to his feet, glaring at me. "You can lie to yourself all you want, Lila. But you cannot lie to me. I know you feel this." He gestures to the air between us, eyes blazing, before he stalks off to the back of the house, leaving us in the front yard.

Lucas won't look at me, so I take another step closer. "Lucas, he's wrong. I don't feel that way about him. And I swear, I was going to push him away. You beat me to it. He totally caught me by surprise—I had no idea he was going to kiss me," I plead, the lump in my throat bigger now, the tears I'm trying so hard to hold back threatening to break through.

He shakes his head at me. "I just don't believe you," he whispers with tears in his own eyes.

I reach out and grab his hand. "Will you just look at me?" I beg, tugging on his hand, willing him to see the truth in my face. "I'm telling you the truth. I swear." My voice finally breaks on the last word.

His jaw clenches and he yanks his hand from my grip. He takes a step back, averting his gaze. "I'm sorry, Lila. I just don't believe anything you say." And he turns and walks away from me.

I sit down on the grass, feeling utterly defeated, and let the tears fall. How the hell did I mess things up this fast? I don't know how long I'm out there crying in the front yard alone before Ashley finds me. She sits down next to me and puts her arm around my slumped frame, pulling me into her comforting embrace. She doesn't say a word, just lets me cry on her shoulder, offering sympathetic sounds and soothing pats on my arm.

"That escalated quickly," I finally say once I pull myself together, wiping my eyes. "Like really quickly. How was it that just two days ago was the first time I saw Lucas in six years? I finally got a second shot and I blew it *again*. And it's all my fault." I let out an incredulous snort and hang my head in shame.

Ash turns to face me. "Is it? I mean, yes, you should have been honest with him from the beginning, but you didn't exactly ask Jamie to kiss you."

I jerk my head up. "How do you know he kissed me?"

"It wasn't hard to figure out; Jamie walked around back in a huff with blood gushing out of his nose." She gives me a sympathetic smile. "And then he colorfully filled in the gaps," she adds with a shrug.

I groan. "He must really hate me too."

"He's just feeling rejected right now. His ego is bruised. He'll live." She gives my arm a squeeze. "If it makes you feel any better, nobody in there believes you wanted to kiss Jamie. We all know how you feel about Lucas."

"Yeah right," I scoff. "You should've heard the lecture Jake and Alex gave me at the bar. They actually accused me of 'dry-humping' Jamie on the dance floor." It sounds so ridiculous I can't help but let out a laugh through my tears.

She raises a brow, grinning herself. "They're just being loyal to their friend. Come on, Lila, those boys have been front and center for the epic crush you've harbored for Lucas your whole entire life. Nobody would think for a second that you would choose Jamie over him."

"Yeah, nobody *but* Lucas." My heart sinks as I say the words.

"Did you ever tell Jamie about Lucas when you were together?"

Valid question. I pause, trying to recall exactly what I told Jamie about my past. "I told him there was a guy back home that broke my heart, but I never got into the gory details. I never even told him Lucas's name. Maybe I should have. I mean, obviously I should have done a lot of things differently here." I open my hands on my knees and look up at her with wet eyes.

She leans her head against mine and we sit in silence for a few minutes.

"Do you think Lucas will ever forgive me?" I whisper to her.

"He'd be a fool not to." She tightens her arm around me. "And that's the truth."

"Thanks, Ash."

Maybe tomorrow I'll wake up and this will have all been a dream.

CHAPTER 15

I t wasn't a dream. I open my eyes and it all comes flooding back to me: the dancing, the kiss, the punch, Lucas walking away. All of it hits me like a tidal wave. I groan silently at the cement block in my stomach and fish for my phone on the nightstand. 8:15 a.m. The bed is empty beside me, which means Ash is either already up or never came to bed. She tucked me in last night after sneaking me downstairs so I wouldn't have to face anyone, then went back upstairs to hang out. I can only imagine what everyone said about the whole disaster. I wonder if Jamie retreated to his room as well.

Shame. Shame. Shame. A chorus loops on and on through my head, like the scene in *Game of Thrones* when the village throws stones at Cersei. *Shame. Shame. Shame.* Ugh, I cannot believe I let this happen.

Today is the Fourth of July, and the last thing I want to do is be social. This disgrace feels all too familiar, like I'm back in high school the Monday after the big blow-up at John's party. Funny how one thing can happen and you're catapulted back through time to the worst day of your life, reliving the same horrific teenage emotions you thought you'd come so far from. You think you're a grownup and this angst is behind you? Ha! Nope, think again. The universe laughs at you and hurls you right back to your humiliation.

I sit up, put my feet on the floor and give myself a little pep talk. *Come on, you're a big girl, you can do this. Get up and face the day.* After throwing my hair in a bun and swapping my PJs for shorts and a tank, I peek my head out into the living room to see if anyone else is awake. Alex is asleep on the couch, but nobody else is around. Friday night, Lucas slept out here on the couch and Alex and Jake slept in the other room. Maybe Lucas went for a run if he's up this early, but I doubt Ash and my brother went with him. I look at the closed door of the other bedroom, a delayed realization hitting me over the head. Ash must have slept in there with my brother. I let out a sound of surprise and a snort-laugh follows. I quickly slap my hand over my mouth, but it's too late—I woke Alex up.

He opens his eyes and sees me frozen in the middle of the room, covering my face. "Li? What are you doing? Ugh, what time is it?" he grumbles and turns over on the couch.

"Umm, how nice of you to give up your bed." I point to the closed door and lift a brow at him.

He grins and sits up, rubbing his eyes. "I wasn't about to be a cockblock."

I wrinkle my nose. "Gah, Alex!" I hiss and sit down next to him, playfully covering my ears.

He scoots closer to me, his expression softening. "How are you feeling today? I wanted to check on you last night, but Ash said you just wanted to go to bed."

"Yeah, I just needed the night to end. Jeez, I can't even believe what happened. It was crazy, Al. I think I seriously fucked things up." I lean against his shoulder. "Was everyone talking about it all night?" I ask, dread pooling in my stomach.

He scoffs. "No, come on now. You know we would never talk about you behind your back."

"Did you see Jamie come inside?" I ask, my voice coming out small.

"For a second. He came in to grab some ice and went straight to his room. Ash and Lucy went in to see if he was okay and I guess he told them what happened and that he was taking the ferry back first thing this morning. Luke really clocked him good, I bet he woke up with a seriously mangled face today," he says, his hand instinctively going to his own nose.

I wince. "He said he's leaving? Shit, I feel terrible. Lucy is his family—if anything, I should be the one leaving."

He looks at me sideways. "Don't be silly, you're not leaving."

"Where is Lucas, anyway? Did he sleep out here with you?" I look at the other couch with a folded-up blanket and pillow on top. It doesn't look like anyone slept on it.

"I'm not sure, I passed out around two a.m. and he hadn't come down here yet. Doesn't look like it, though," he says, following my line of sight. "Maybe he's upstairs? I need coffee anyway. Bad." He groans and stands up to stretch.

"Agree." I nod and follow him up the stairs.

Lucas isn't in the kitchen, but Lucy and Thomas are sitting at the counter drinking coffee.

I feel my face grow hot with embarrassment when

170

their eyes fall on me. "Good morning," I say timidly, averting my gaze.

"Oh good, there's coffee," Alex says with relief and reaches for the pot. Lucy must have dug it out from somewhere since I didn't see it here yesterday. He pulls two mugs down from the cabinet, fills them both and hands me one.

I gratefully accept.

"How are you, Lila?" Lucy asks me, sympathy washing across her face.

"Been better, thanks." I give her a small, nervous smile. "Have you seen Lucas?"

Silence. The moment stretches. She and Thomas look at each other, then back to me with pity in their eyes. "He left about half an hour ago. Said he was catching the jitney back home," she finally answers.

My face falls and I look over at Alex, who's staring at them, confusion clouding his features.

"He what?" he asks.

Thomas nods silently.

"I'm so sorry," Lucy says softly, wincing.

I collapse on a stool, my shoulder slumped in defeat. I feel nauseous. I can't believe he just went home without a word. "And Jamie?" I dare to ask her, although I anticipate the answer is the same.

"Took the first ferry back to Rhode Island," she says, a pained look on her face.

"Wow, can I clear a house." I laugh without mirth. "Shit," I mutter to myself and drop my head into my hands. I take a steadying breath to hold back the tears threatening to break free.

Alex walks over and puts a hand on my shoulder,

offering me comfort that I probably don't even deserve. "It'll be okay. You guys will figure it out."

I can't bring myself to believe his words. Right now it feels all too much like I'm back in that parking lot in high school, losing Lucas all over again.

All I want to do is climb back into bed, so when Lucy and Thomas say they're going to the bakery to pick up breakfast for everyone (everyone who didn't flee at first light, that is), I head back downstairs to do just that. Alex goes out back to do laps in the pool to "work off all the beer he's been guzzling before his middle-age paunch catches up with him."

I descend the last step and enter the living area at the same moment Ashley opens the door of Jake's room. If I wasn't so heartbroken right now, I would probably double over with laughter at the sight of her. She looks like a deer caught in headlights. Her blonde hair is sticking up all over, last night's makeup is smudged in black circles under her eyes and she's wearing a tiny tank top that I recognize from high school—and no pants. I fling my hands up to cover my eyes as she gives a little yelp and backtracks into the room, not realizing my brother is standing behind her as she knocks right into his shirtless chest.

"Ouch! Ash, what the hell?" He grabs her shoulders to steady her and peers around her, looking to see what's got her so spooked. "Oh shit, Lila. Um, hi." His face immediately flushes crimson.

With my hands still covering my eyes, I walk straight into the back of the couch, the cut on my knee from surfing catching the hard edge of the arm. "Ah, fuck!" I lower one arm to grab my knee while still covering my face with the other. I'm hit with a wave of hopelessness so overwhelming that I just collapse on the couch and let out a wail.

Ash and Jake both come running over. "Shit, Li. Are you okay? I'm so sorry! Please don't be upset with us." She crouches down in front of me, her eyes wide.

The sobs are coming uncontrollably now, and I'm finding it hard to catch my breath.

"Jesus, Lila. It's not that big of a deal," my brother says, a whispered curse coming a beat later, which I can only imagine is from Ash elbowing him, since I can't see clearly through the deluge of water gushing out of my eyes.

"Lila, breathe," Ash says, trying to coach me through the panic attack I seem to be having.

I follow her lead, drawing in long breaths and slowly exhaling them out. In, out, in, out.

"Hey Lila, have you seen my goggles?" Alex yells as he bounds down the stairs, and stops short when he takes in the scene. "What's going on?" He asks with alarm when he sees me hunched over on the couch with Ash and Jake kneeling at my feet.

Jake reaches up to rub the back of his neck. "Well, Lila just caught Ash sneaking out of my room, and seems to be having a fucking meltdown about it," he says, annoyance sharpening his tone.

"You idiot. It's not that," I wheeze out when I'm finally able to suck in some air.

"Lucas left this morning." Alex clarifies for me. "*And* Jamie."

My brother blows out a breath. Ash is speechless.

I wipe my eyes and nod miserably. "Yup."

"Sorry, I really thought that was about us," Jake says, his expression now softened.

"No, no." I shake my head and look up at them. A laugh escapes my lips when I notice Ashley's bare legs and realize she completely forgot she's in her underwear.

She follows my gaze and slaps her hands on her bare thighs to cover them, then bursts out laughing herself.

"I'm not mad," I say, welcoming the brief moment of comedic relief, even though it barely eclipses the cloud of sorrow parked in my chest. "Although, maybe you want to grab some pants for Ash?" My gaze slides to my brother, whose eyes bulge when he registers Ash's outfit.

The flush now spreads to his ears before he starts laughing, too. He runs back into the room to grab a pair of pajama pants and tosses them at her. Alex chuckles to himself and turns away to rummage through his bag for his goggles as she pulls them on.

Fully clothed, she sits next to me and grabs my hand. "I thought for sure you were pissed when you saw me in the doorway," she says and shakes her head, grinning. Then she narrows her eyes as she mutters under her breath, "I can't believe they both ran away like little bitches."

"I know this is probably not the best time for this conversation," my brother says to me. "And you probably think I'm the biggest hypocrite here," he adds, "but I don't want you thinking there's been any sneaking around behind your back. This just happened." He gestures between him and Ash.

She nods emphatically. "It's true. The other night at the bar, something just shifted between us. Then we went for a run the next day, and we've just been having so much fun together ever since." She smiles at him, and he meets her gaze with the happiest expression I've ever seen on my brother's face.

"It's okay, really. We've noticed, believe me," I say, and jut my chin toward Alex, who watches with amusement.

"Yeah guys, we aren't blind," he adds, rolling his eyes at them.

They look sheepish as they continue making googly eyes at each other.

"At least this trip brought one couple together," I say, and lean back into the couch with a sigh. "I'm happy for you guys. After the yuck factor, of course." I shiver, shaking the image of them naked together out of my head. "But really, I am." I smile at them, trying to convey my sincerity. "I just wish my own life wasn't simultaneously going to shit."

Chapter 16

Winter 2016

Winter 2016

I hear knocking on the door and wake with a jolt. I orient myself to my surroundings—the hotel room, the salty breeze coming through the open balcony door—and remember where I am. Mexico. Right, the wedding. I must have dozed off waiting for my luggage. Damn, how long was I out for? The clock on the nightstand tells me only twenty minutes. Phew, I could have easily slept right through the rehearsal dinner. Traveling, plus my heightened emotional state is draining all of my energy.

A second knock forces me up off the bed. I wipe the drool from my face and swipe at the mascara I know has run under my eyes. After tipping the porter, who looks not a day over fifteen, I quickly unpack my suitcase and change into a cute sundress I bought specifically for this trip. I slip on a pair of leather sandals, twist my hair up into a bun and head back downstairs.

My empty stomach churns with nerves as I give myself another pep talk in the elevator. *You can do this, Lila, no big deal.* I try not to think about how awkward it'll be when I finally see him. Lucas and I haven't had much contact since he left me in Montauk on the Fourth of July. He wouldn't answer my texts or calls for weeks after, no matter how many times I tried to contact him and apologize.

Alex or Jake must have had enough of my moping and finally said something to him, even though they both swore they weren't getting involved. Exactly four weeks to the day after July Fourth, I got a text from him that read, ***Sorry, it just wasn't going to work out. Take care of yourself.*** Twelve words. That's all I got —twelve words.

Ash and I both dissected every single one of those twelve words a million and a half times. We came to the conclusion he must have temporarily gone insane to think that was a sufficient response after bailing without a goodbye, and then ghosting me for weeks after. I know I fucked up and lied about Jamie, but given our history and the numerous attempts at an apology, his behavior struck me as particularly harsh. How could he not think I deserved more than that text?

Alex and Jake both agreed as well, but they reminded me how they'd made it clear from the start they didn't "want to hear about it if things go south" (I believe those were the exact words my brother used). And they shouldn't have had to—they were right. We're grownups now. But to be totally honest, I'm genuinely hurt that Lucas could just write me off like that. Hurt that he would think the worst of me and not give me a chance to explain. Hurt that he could ignore all my attempts at an apology whatsoever, or to talk it through and make things right. And so very fucking hurt that he could just move on so easily after everything he said about wanting to give us another shot.

Okay Lila, no more of this. I give my head a shake, trying to clear any bad thoughts of the past. I do one last check of my hair in the reflection of the elevator door, and smooth out any residual wrinkles on my dress from the suitcase. As the door opens to the lobby, I flinch backwards when I see a pair of all-too-familiar green eyes staring back at me.

"Lila, hi," Lucas says awkwardly, stepping aside for me to exit the elevator.

However, I'm stuck in place; my feet don't seem to be moving. I open my mouth, but no sound comes out as I look at the petite blonde next to him, holding on to his arm. I feel my eyes almost pop out of my head when they register the huge rock on her ring finger. She looks back at me with annoyance, clearly miffed I'm not exiting the elevator in a timely fashion. She must be a hundred pounds soaking wet, with large blue eyes and a cropped tank top showing off her tiny waist. I pry my gaze from her ring and back to her face. Wait a second, I recognize that face. Chloe fucking Bailey from high school. My stomach drops to my knees. I must still be sleeping; this has to be a dream. A very bad dream.

My eyes flick back to Lucas, and he sees the understanding pass across my features. He averts his gaze. His face is turning redder by the second, the flush creeping to his ears and down his neck. I'm guessing my own face looks pretty colorful right about now as well.

The elevator doors begin to close, and the blinged-out hand reaches out to stop them. "Are you getting off?" she asks with irritation.

I snap out of my trance. "Yes, yes. Um, sorry," I reply as I step into the lobby. I can actually feel the awkwardness slap me in the face. "Lucas, hi," I say to him as I watch him look everywhere but my face. "Did you, uh, just get here?" I stammer, not knowing what the hell to say.

"Yes. Yeah, just got here," he mumbles. Apparently he has also lost the ability to speak coherently. His blonde companion steps into the elevator as he stays rooted in place while this cringeworthy moment stretches on for what feels like forever, each of us shifting uncomfortably and stuttering broken sentences.

The elevator doors try to close again. "Are you coming up or not, Luke?" she asks after reaching out to stop them a second time.

His face snaps to her, looking startled, as if he forgot she was even there. "Oh, uh, yeah. Lila, you remember Chloe, right? Chloe, Lila." He gestures between us.

"Yeah, hi." Chloe eyes me from inside the elevator.

I do my best to offer her a polite smile, still permanently paralyzed.

Lucas steps in to join her with a pained expression on his face and finally meets my gaze. "We're going up to change real quick, but will see you later?"

I swallow the lump in my throat and can only manage a nod at this point, as the elevator doors finally close in my face.

What the hell? I walk to the nearest bench and sit down, trying to calm my racing heart. Lucas is *engaged*? To Chloe from high school? How is this happening?

When did they even start dating? And why the hell is everyone getting engaged so fast all of a sudden? My thoughts are a whirlwind as I try to beat back the threatening panic attack. I don't know how long I sit there counting my breaths before Ash finds me.

"Lila, there you are! We've been waiting for you. What are you doing?" she asks, her voice raising an octave as she clocks my state of distress. Her face falls as she instantly connects the dots. "Shit, you saw him."

I look up at her through wet eyes. "How could you not tell me he's engaged?" I croak.

She takes a seat next to me, her gaze unwavering. "I swear I had no idea. This just happened like a couple days ago. Apparently he didn't tell anyone—he said he didn't want to *'steal our thunder.'*" She says this while making air quotes. "I found out when we just saw them now." She puts a hand on my back. "Of course I would've told you," she says with emphasis.

"But you had to know they were seeing each other. You had to know he was bringing a plus-one to your wedding," I say, shaking my head with disbelief.

"I thought it was just a stupid rebound hookup, and I didn't want to upset you for no reason. I never thought it would last more than a few dates. And no, I really had no idea she was coming to the wedding. He asked Jake if he could bring her just last week, and that coward didn't even tell me, thinking I would flip out about an extra guest. *And* tell you, and start even more drama. This is all a surprise to me too, I swear." She says this with such sincerity on her open face that it's hard not to believe her.

I purse my lips. "I will kill my brother." I stand up abruptly, rage swirling in my chest. "He knew the whole car ride here from the airport and didn't think to share this information?" I pace back and forth, wringing my hands.

Ash shoots to her feet after me, her eyes wide with alarm. "Please, please don't. I really want my wedding to be perfect, Li. I know that's a tall order right now when it's looking more like a shitshow. This is a shock to me, too. But please don't murder my soon-to-be-husband before he can walk down the aisle," she pleads and grabs my arm.

I stop short when I see the distress on her face. I sit back on the bench and bury my head in my hands. "This is insanity. How can this be happening right now? It's been like, what, four months? How can he be engaged in four fucking months?" I groan, eyes sliding to hers.

She gives me a sheepish glance back, knowing she's also guilty of this so-called crime.

I let out a snort. "You know what I mean!" I say, rolling my eyes dramatically at her. "But really, is this the fucking trend now?"

"I know, I'm so, so sorry, Lila," she says softly.

We sit in silence for a moment. I draw in a few deep breaths, blow them out, and wipe my eyes. "Okay, okay. You're right, this is your wedding. And I'm not going to ruin it. I'm a big girl, I can handle it." I reach up to check that my bun is still intact. I stand up and straighten my dress, smoothing out the nonexistent wrinkles.

She eyes me critically from her perch on the bench. "Really? Just like that? You're okay?" she asks, her lifted brows indicate she's not quite buying my swift change of heart.

I give her a curt nod. "I came here to be your maid of honor, and that's what I'm going to do," I say. "I'll kill my brother after your honeymoon," I add with a fake smile.

Her shoulders collapse with relief. She stands up and

pulls me in for a hug. "Thank you. I love you so much," she whispers in my ear.

I pull back, locking eyes with her. "But I swear to God, if someone else I know gets engaged in less than a freaking year, I will seriously lose my shit."

She rears back with a laugh, and with one last squeeze of my hand, leads me out the sliding doors.

Jake is holding court outside at the bar with both sets of parents. After kissing everyone hello and ordering a much-needed margarita, I sidle up next to him and casually step on his flip-flopped foot with my sandal, easing pressure down little by little.

"Rumor has it you have been holding back some information that I would like to have known prior to this event, big brother," I say under my breath while slowly increasing the pressure of my foot. My eyes slide to his and our gazes lock, mine subtly narrowing at him.

He gallantly tries to smooth his features to conceal any hint of pain, doing his best to look as though his pinkie toe isn't screaming in agony right now. "Just trying to keep the peace for my wedding weekend," he casually responds with a faint smile on his lips.

I press down harder now, and his impenetrable demeanor starts to crack. He winces and breaks eye contact. I smirk with victory at winning our staring contest.

"The only reason I'm not murdering you right now is because Ashley is my best friend and we've been dreaming of our weddings since we were six years old," I murmur to him under my breath, attempting to keep my voice low and even.

I pause and glance around, making sure we're not attracting anyone else's attention.

"But just know that if that wasn't the case, I would indeed be wreaking havoc on more than your foot right now," I say while giving him my best murderous glare. I quickly press down my hardest one last time, really squishing his toe to the floor before easing my foot off completely.

"Noted," he croaks, and clears his throat, recovering. He rubs the back of his neck, looking contrite, and leans in closer to me. "I'm sorry, Li. Really. I honestly did just find out myself, and I didn't know how to tell you."

His expression looks sincere, and maybe this was an honest attempt to keep the peace, but I really wish I was forewarned. I can't help but feel completely ambushed. However, I promised Ash I wouldn't ruin her wedding, and I plan on keeping my word.

I offer him a curt smile and nod, then I grab my drink and move to the other end of the bar to sit with my parents. It takes every ounce of willpower I have not to gulp my drink down in one sip. This is going to be one hell of a weekend.

CHAPTER 17

The hotel has set up one long table on the patio next to the pool for the rehearsal dinner. The staff leads us to our seats, and I can't help but marvel at the beauty of this place. It is truly a perfect setting for the occasion. The reflection of the twinkle lights strung from the palm trees sets the pool ablaze, and the ocean crashing on the beach serenades us. If I wasn't such a tornado of thoughts and emotions right now, I might be able to appreciate it better.

I take my seat next to Ashley at one end. The seat on my other side is empty; apparently Alex's flight was delayed and he won't be arriving until late tonight. Lucas and Chloe sit down across the table from us. I give them a faint smile and try to calm my nerves, reminding myself of my role for the weekend.

The waiter comes over and hands out flutes of champagne, which I gratefully accept.

Chloe goes to reach for her glass, but Lucas gives her a look and blocks her hand with his own. "Oh right, whoops," she says a little too loud, causing me to look up and catch her eye. She gives me a wink across the table, and the bottom falls out from my stomach.

I blink slowly, registering what just happened. No way, not possible.

Ash must have witnessed this display, and her inability to think before she speaks causes her to blurt out, "Oh my God, are you pregnant?" She slaps a hand over her mouth the second the words escape her lips.

My own jaw drops to my salad plate, and the whole table quiets immediately, all eyes on Lucas and Chloe.

Lucas's face turns beet red and his eyes go wide as they shoot to mine.

I'm frozen in place. I can't speak, I can't close my mouth, I can only stare at him in shock with my mouth agape, praying for it not to be true.

"Guilty," Chloe says with a sheepish shrug of her bony shoulder. She grabs Lucas's hand on the table and intertwines their fingers.

He quickly breaks our eye contact, averting his gaze from mine. The rigid set to his shoulders and tense line of his jaw suggests he did not exactly want to disclose this information, and is less than thrilled that it's now public knowledge.

"We wanted to wait to announce because we didn't want to overshadow your weekend," she says to Ash and Jake, her shining eyes and the faint smirk on her lips suggesting otherwise.

Ash smacks my leg under the table, her jaw now mirroring my own.

My brother clears his throat. "Wow. Well, congrats man." He gets up and walks around the table to hug Lucas, with the rest of the guests following suit.

Lucas has still yet to say a word. His nervous smile looks more like a grimace with each congrats he receives.

I still seem to be having trouble closing my mouth.

Ash also seems frozen in shock. She slowly turns her head in my direction and when her eyes find mine, I read in them her wordless plea for me not to make a scene—for the second time today.

Across the table, my brother motions for Ash to get up and join him in congratulating the happy couple. She obliges, and I am powerless as I watch her stand and shuffle over to them, leaving me alone in my seat.

"Well you guys sure move fast," she says, leaning in to give Lucas a hug.

I can only manage to squeak out a small grunt in their direction, which gets lost in the loud sea of well-wishers. I glance down at my watch, calculating how long till I can make an acceptable escape.

I down the rest of my champagne and signal the waiter for another. When Ash sits back down in her seat next to me, she presses her elbow into my own. A full glass appears next to me, and I give the waiter a nod of gratitude.

The rest of dinner passes by in a blur. The apps are served, the alcohol flows, the fathers give speeches, the mothers shed tears, and Lucas avoids my gaze throughout all of it. In fact, he actively avoids turning his head in my direction at all. I am insanely thankful that my speech is not until tomorrow; I don't think I could string together anything coherent right now.

Finally, the main courses are cleared, and I decide that I've literally had all I can handle. I slip away from the table and head down the path to the beach. I take off my sandals, toss them in the sand and walk down to the water. The sensation of the cool waves on my toes brings me back to reality and after a few deep breaths of the salty ocean air, I feel my shoulders finally start to retreat from my ears.

This will all be over in a couple of days, I remind myself, repeating it over and over—a mantra soothing my frayed nerves. *Just hang in. You can do this, Lila.*

I sense someone approaching and I inwardly groan to myself, already beginning to grieve my treasured moment of solitude. I turn around and see Lucas walking toward me. Ugh, what could he possibly want? My face must mirror that thought because he stops a few feet away, uncertainty playing across his features. I cock my head in question, not trusting my voice right now.

He swallows. "I was hoping we could talk for a sec," he says after a beat.

"Talk?" My eyebrows retreat into my hairline.

"Yeah. Talk."

I stare at him blankly.

"Exchange words. Also called a conversation?" he says.

I give him a slight shrug and turn back to look out at the water. What is there left to say? He's clearly moved on. And fast. Message delivered, loud and clear.

He takes a step forward. "Can you at least look at me?" he says softly, his voice pleading.

I whip back around. "Fine. Talk. Say whatever it is you feel the need to say to me, Lucas."

He sighs and scrubs a hand down his face. A typical Lucas mannerism. I feel a sharp pang in my chest when I realize he's not mine to know anymore; never really was, if I'm honest with myself. I tear my eyes away from his and try to focus on the crashing surf, the immensity of the ocean, the shape of the moon—anything to keep me from looking into his eyes. The eyes I dreamed of every night for the last four months, and a lifetime before that.

"I know this is all probably a shock to you. And I'm sorry you had to find out like that. I really didn't mean to ambush you here, but it all just happened so fast. I thought about calling you a million times over the last few months, but I just didn't know how to tell you. So I kept putting it off, and then time got away from me, and here we are." He splays his hands open.

All I can manage is a nod, still not trusting my voice.

"This is the part where you speak," he says quietly, gesturing for me to respond.

I close my eyes and sigh. "What do you want me to say?"

"Anything. Just say something. What are you thinking, Lila?"

"Chloe seems great. I hope you guys are very happy together. Congratulations." I twist my mouth into a smile, then turn around and walk away from him.

"Wait, Lila!" he calls after me. "Can you please just talk to me here?" He reaches out and grabs my arm.

I shake him off. "I don't understand what you want me to say, Lucas! My world is a little rocked right now, okay? You shut me out for months, making me feel like I was at fault, and now I find out you've actually been pretty fucking busy the whole time."

He blows out a long breath. "I'm sorry, it was all so unexpected."

"Whatever. It is what it is." I wince at the expression, knowing it's a pet peeve of his.

"You know I hate that expression."

I glare at him, feeling a tornado of rage swirling in my

chest. "Well? It is, isn't it? You chose to leave that morning without a word, and then never answer any of my calls or texts. You chose to start dating Chloe, and you chose to fucking propose to her, *impregnate her*, and I've barely had time to unpack my overnight bag from Montauk!"

He flinches at the venom in my tone. "I get that you're pissed. You have every right to be. Look, the truth is that the night I came home on the Fourth of July, I was so torn up inside. I felt betrayed. I really believed you had something going on with Jamie, and that kiss sent me off the rails. I know I was being dramatic by leaving that morning without saying goodbye, but I was so humiliated and just couldn't face you. I was totally crushed. As soon as I got back home, I went to the bar and started drinking. Heavily. After God knows how long, sitting alone in a dark bar, replaying the events of the weekend, going over and over in my mind what a chump I was, Chloe came in with her friends. I was sad, tired and drunk, and one thing led to another and I went home with her." He cringes as the words leave his lips, and looks down at the sand.

I wince at this onslaught of information and shoot my hand up to stop him. "I don't need to know the gory details, okay?"

He nods. "I just want to explain how it happened. You deserve to know the truth."

I let out a snort, and he continues. "I woke up to a bunch of calls and texts from everyone still in Montauk. I was hungover and ashamed of what I had done. Both leaving with no explanation like a coward, and sleeping with someone the very same day. I felt horrible, like the worst kind of hypocrite. I didn't want to talk to anyone, so I just retreated into myself. Physically and emotionally. I was hurt, Lila. I was so excited about finally reconnecting with you—that night we had together was amazing. I thought about what it would be like to see you again for so long. And then shortly after, *so* shortly after, it all just blew up in my face. I felt blindsided, like the wind was knocked out of me." He stops and takes a breath. The vulnerability on his face and in his words throw me off balance.

To my horror, I feel tears pricking my eyes, threatening to escape. I turn away before a traitorous one slips out, trying discreetly to wipe it away.

His eyes catch my movement, and a flash of emotion washes over his face. "I'm *so* sorry, Lila. I was jealous and stupid. I should have stayed and let you explain instead of running away. And then I felt so ashamed for sleeping with Chloe so soon. I just didn't know what to say to you. I knew that if we talked I would have to tell you the truth, and I just couldn't bear to hurt you like that. So, I was a fucking spineless chicken and hid from it all," he says, his voice strained and his shoulders crumpled with defeat.

My tears flow freely now, and I'm unable to stop them. I don't even bother wiping them off my cheeks; I just let them fall. I can't believe what I'm hearing. This whole time he pushed me away because of *his* behavior and not *mine*. I remember the weight of the crushing guilt I've been carrying for months and my mind struggles to process the fact that this radio silence from him actually hasn't been all my fault.

"Say something, Lila. Please!" he says, his hands in fists at his sides.

"This is so *fucked*," I yell at him.

He steps back, caught off guard by my outburst.

I press a hand to my chest to try and still my hammering heart. "This whole time I felt horrible for lying to you about Jamie, and the longer you shut me out, the more guilty I felt. I really believed I was responsible for our breakup, if you can even call it that. Jesus, Lucas, I felt like a terrible human being! The hope that one day you would wake up and forgive me was a constant ache I carried around for weeks. And this whole time, you avoiding me wasn't even my fault?" I run my hands through my hair, not believing this is happening.

"Of course it wasn't your fault. Yes, you should've told me the truth, and honestly, I don't entirely regret punching Jamie in the face, but I see how silly and jealous I acted now. I would do anything to go back to that day and not get on that jitney. I would do anything to take it back, Lila. I want you to know that." He grabs my hand, pulling me to meet his red-rimmed eyes.

I shake my head, not even knowing what to do with all of this. "Okay, so fine, you slept with Chloe that day. You really think I would have just cut you off? We had two days together after *six years* of not even speaking. I would have forgiven you! But you didn't even give me that choice to make." I groan. How could he think I would be so cold and unforgiving? And not to mention hypocritical.

Misery washes over his face as he draws a breath and blows it out. "After a few weeks of self-loathing, I finally started to get up my nerve to talk to you, reminding myself of the kind and understanding person you are. I started to believe that maybe you would have forgiven me. Your compassion is one of my favorite things about you. It always has been, Lila. It took a while to remember that through the fog of self-hatred and shame." He scrubs a hand over his jaw, steeling himself before he continues. "But then Chloe told me she was pregnant. And I just knew there was no redeeming myself after that. My poor judgment led to some pretty life-altering decisions. And I had to step up and take responsibility for my actions. I would never leave my kid the way my dad left me. I knew we were done for good then, and it completely gutted me. I just couldn't face you. I had to be steadfast in my decision, and I was terrified that after one look at you, my resolve would be thrown out the window." He sighs heavily, studying my reaction to his words. He slowly reaches out and touches my cheek, sending a jolt of electricity down my face as he wipes away a tear.

I cannot tear my eyes from his. Our chemistry is palpable in this moment. We stand there staring at each other for what feels like an eternity. All of a sudden he leans in to place his lips on mine, and I am unable to stop him. The second we touch, I feel the same fireworks coursing through my body that I always feel with us. He completely consumes my senses and the rest of the world fades away. I briefly get lost in him as he deepens the kiss, his hands tangling in my hair. A moan escapes deep in his throat, which slaps me back to reality and I pull back, covering my mouth with my hands.

"What the hell was that?" I take a step back, eyes wide.

He looks as startled as I am, not knowing what to say as his hands fall to his sides. "I'm sorry," he finally whispers, looking down at his feet. "I'm really, really sorry."

My head is so fogged with lust and anger and shock that I can barely form a coherent thought. "I don't know what the fuck is going on here"—I gesture between us —"but I cannot be anywhere near you right now," I say and run back up the beach in the direction of the hotel.

This time he lets me go.

I pass our table, which is empty of people. Only the remnants of the drinks and dessert that I missed are left. The outdoor bar is also void of our party, and I exhale a sigh of relief that everyone must have retreated to their rooms for the night. All I want to do is get into bed and hide under the covers, but I still have to find Ash and do my maid-of-honor, night-before sleepover duty.

Lucas's words play on a loop in my brain. I can't believe this whole time I truly believed I was the cause of his disappearance, and it was really because of Chloe all along.

I just want this day to end. When I get to the lobby, the cold marble floor reminds me that I left my shoes on the beach. Ugh, screw it. I'll find them tomorrow—there is no way I am going back there right now.

I furiously press the button for the elevator, praying to God to let me slip upstairs unnoticed. My mind is a freaking cyclone, and the last thing I want is to talk to any of our family members right now. I hear my mother's laugh and without thinking hide behind a large potted palm tree next to the elevator bank. She walks out of the bar and in the opposite direction from me toward the ladies' room, and I press a hand to my chest, releasing the breath I didn't realize I was holding.

As I'm about to exit my hiding place, Chloe emerges from the same door my mother just went in, and I flatten myself back against the wall, praying the shadows conceal me. My eyes pop out of my head as she approaches a waiter carrying a tray of freshly poured champagne flutes and plucks one off the tray, giving him a flirty smile. She quickly looks over her shoulder before she downs the whole flute in one gulp.

Again, my jaw unhinges itself. Am I hallucinating?

What the hell is she doing? Either she's lying about this baby or she's putting Lucas's unborn child's well-being in jeopardy. Either way, she's not helping my already negative opinion of her. My preconceived notions about this woman are pretty much solidified. She does not deserve one ounce of Lucas's love or devotion.

After she disappears outside, probably to scrounge up some more illicit alcohol, I collect myself and emerge from behind my palm tree. Luckily I make it into the elevator and up to the room undetected, muttering to myself in disbelief the whole time. I fish the key card out from where I stashed it in my bra, my hand shaking as I try to unlock the door to my room. Finally giving up after three misses, I sit down on the floor of the hallway right in front of the door. Just as I lean my head back against the hard surface, the door flings open and I fall backwards onto the carpet, Ash's confused face peering down at me.

"There you are! Jesus, Lila, where have you been?" She crouches to my level with concern in her big blue eyes. "Where are your shoes?"

I fling my hands over my face. "You have no idea," I groan.

"Well here, get up off the floor and come inside." She reaches out to help me up.

I oblige and follow her in, only to flop myself down on the bed. "How did you get in here, anyway?" I ask her, remembering now that I never gave her a key.

"The maid let me in," she says with a shrug. Leave it to Ash to be resourceful. "Now are you going to tell me what happened?" she asks, not letting me off the hook.

I squeeze my eyes shut and relay the whole story. All of it. Everything Lucas said to me on the beach, the kiss, and what I saw Chloe do in the lobby.

She lets me finish, her eyes growing by the second, and lets out a long whistle. "Holy shit. Holy shit! I *knew* there had to be a reason he disappeared on you like that. Lucas totally ghosting you after your history together didn't sit right with me. I just knew there was more to the story," she exclaims, slapping my arm. After a beat, the excitement in her eyes dims and she looks at me with sympathy. "Are you gonna tell him what you saw?" she asks softly.

I snort at her. "Oh sure, the jilted lover he rejected is just going to nonchalantly go up to him and say, 'By the way, the woman you pledged your life to is a liar,'" I scoff with a roll of my eyes.

She purses her lips while she thinks about my words. "Fair point. But still, he thinks he's doing the right thing here by sticking with her. And with his family history, this is some deep-rooted shit. He can't marry her!" she says, her tone animated again.

"Maybe she really is pregnant and just doesn't care," I say with a slight shrug, only half believing it myself. "Who the hell knows, Ash? People drink when they're pregnant all the time."

She cocks her head. "Yeah, okay—they take a sip or two of their husband's beer, fine. They don't stealthily chug a whole champagne flute in one gulp."

Her words do have merit, but still, I don't see myself coming out on top here if I open my mouth to Lucas.

"Ugh, why is this happening? I wish I never even saw it. Can't I pretend I never saw it?" I plead, throwing an arm over my eyes.

"You can, but I know you, and regardless of what an ass he's been, and he has been quite an ass, I know keeping quiet will eat you up inside," she says, tugging my arm away from my face.

I let out a groan, knowing she's right.

"Just, maybe don't say anything yet...not before my wedding ceremony?" she adds, scrunching her nose at me.

I stifle an eye roll and laugh at what is becoming a popular plea from her not to ruin her wedding. "Yeah, yeah." I wave my hand in her direction. Tired of my own drama, I realize I kind of bailed on dinner tonight. I turn my head to look at her. "I'm sorry I missed the end of dinner. Did anything exciting happen?" I ask, eager to hear about something besides Lucas and Chloe.

"Just our mothers getting wasted and bawling their eyes out about us all officially becoming family. Oh, and your mom kept trying to speak Spanish to the waiter; he wasn't refreshing her ice glass quick enough and she kept barking at him, 'Yellow! Yellow!' It was quite amusing."

A snort escapes my lips. "Sounds about right," I reply, unable to feel my usual secondhand embarrassment at this familiar scenario of my mother mispronouncing the Spanish word for "ice" on top of the onslaught of other emotions present. "Sadly, she'll probably be doing that all weekend." I offer an apologetic smile.

Ash laughs and shakes her head at me. She leans in for a hug. "I'm so sorry, Li. I know you're upset. But look at the bright side, it really wasn't your fault. You can finally stop beating yourself up about the whole Jamie thing." She leans back and looks up at me, her eyes hopeful.

"I guess. But the end result is the same either way," I say with a frown.

"We'll see," she says. "It's not over yet." She gives me

a knowing look. "Now let's get ready for bed. I need my beauty sleep. I'm *getting married tomorrow*!"

I can't help but grin at her. As crappy as I feel right now, I am so happy for her and my brother. I feel so lucky that my best friend is actually going to be my sister. And as much as I want to crawl under the bed and hide for the rest of the weekend, I'm here to be her maid of honor, and I steel my resolve to carry out the job, no matter what it takes.

CHAPTER 18

I wake up to Ash blasting "Going to the Chapel" on her phone. I grab her vacant pillow and smush it on top of my head. Exhaustion hangs like a fog in my brain; I feel like I haven't slept at all. Last night comes rushing back to me in waves. No, more like one big tsunami. The pit in my stomach grows as I replay the events of the night in my mind. How can I possibly face Lucas today? Then I remember I'm here for Ash and Jake and fling the covers off, determined to power through. I will throw myself into being the best maid of honor ever. I will show up in full for my best friend and my brother if it's the last thing I do. Lucas and Chloe be damned.

Ash has laid out a whole slew of beauty products on top of the vanity in the bathroom. We slather our faces with hydrating masks and pop de-puffing patches under our eyes, which I am utterly grateful for considering the bags and dark circles under mine this morning. Our mothers show up with coffee and croissants, and soon after we all head down to the salon for our makeup and hair appointments. I sit back in my chair and sip my first well-deserved mimosa of the morning, trying my hardest to relax while my stylist pokes and prods my head and face. I say a prayer of thanks that this is a small wedding and there isn't a frenzy of women primping all around us right now. It feels nice for this to be an intimate moment, just us and our moms.

I look over at Ash and catch her eye in the mirror.

She grins at me and gives me a wink.

I give her one in return and raise my mimosa in a private gesture of cheers. Seems like both of us are welcoming the calm before the storm.

She blows me a kiss before turning her attention back to my mother, who's giving her tips on places to visit on her honeymoon in Italy.

I can't help but smile at how happy and at peace she looks, and gratitude fills my chest that my best friend is so amazing. My brother is one lucky guy, and I am overjoyed for them.

Alex comes in a little while later with a bouquet of roses and a large iced coffee. He hands Ash the flowers and tells her she's the perfect bride. Then he turns to me, hands me the iced coffee and pulls me in for a hug. "Jake filled me in on Lucas," he whispers in my ear. "I thought maybe you'd need a boost to get through the day?" he adds as he pulls back, eyeing me with sympathy.

I am overcome with emotion at his thoughtfulness, and I throw my arms back around him and squeeze tight, trying with all my might to beat back the tears threatening to slip out. *I will not cry today*, I repeat to myself. Well, over Lucas anyway—I'm guaranteed to cry during my maid-of-honor speech, but I try to push the thought out of my head. The idea of standing up to do my speech later will only add to my already frayed nerves.

"God, I love you. I forgive you for abandoning me last night," I say, releasing him from my grip and swatting his arm.

He steps back in mock surrender. "Blame Delta!" he says with a smirk. His face turns serious as he leans in again. "Really though, Li, I am sorry I wasn't there for you. That must have been hard. And for the record, I had no idea they were engaged." By the look on his face, I know he means it.

I shake his apology off with a wave of my hand. "I appreciate it, but it's fine. This is Ash and Jake's day, and I don't want to ruin it with my drama," I say with finality, tabling the topic for the time being.

He looks at me with skepticism, but lets it go on hearing my tone. He turns to the group. "Okay, well, I have to get back to the men's side," he says with a wink. "You ladies look stunning. See you out there." And with a kiss on the cheek for the bride and both our moms, he's gone.

I close my eyes and take a grateful sip of my much-needed coffee, smiling to myself at how well he knows me. At least I have him to help me get through today. I exhale with a sigh of relief.

After hair and makeup is done, we head into the bridal suite to put our dresses on and have more champagne. The hotel has laid out a spread of snacks for us, which I am insanely thankful for after my meager breakfast earlier this morning. Two mimosas on just half of a croissant could be dangerous. My stomach has been growling for the last hour now. I shove a mini chicken salad sandwich in my mouth, and my stomach lurches, threatening to retaliate. *Get it together, Lila.* I take a few deep, calming breaths and distract myself by helping Ash with the straps on her ridiculously high Jimmy Choo sandals she got just for today.

The wedding coordinator pops her head in to give us a ten-minute warning.

Ash grabs my hands, her face breaking into a wide grin. "I can't believe I'm getting married. To your *brother!*" she says, accompanied by her little signature squeal.

"Ew," I say in mock disgust. We both laugh. "Just kidding. I'm so happy for you. I can't imagine a better match for him. Now we really will be sisters." I wrap my arms around her. "You ready to do this thing?" I ask, checking my watch.

She nods with tears in her eyes.

Her mom fluffs her veil, and I take a step back, soaking it all in. She is truly breathtaking. Her dress is an off-white satin that hugs her slim silhouette, with a plunging neckline and spaghetti straps that accentuate her toned shoulders and criss-cross down her back. Her long blonde hair hangs in loose waves topped with a minimalist veil flowing out of a thin rhinestone headband. I can't wait to see my brother's face when his eyes land on her.

We walk out into the vestibule to where Ash's dad is waiting, and he chokes up when he sees her. The song that is my cue starts, and I take one last breath before I step outside to begin my walk down the aisle. The ceremony is on a private stone patio overlooking the beach with potted palms lining the perimeter and twinkle lights strung between. My pulse goes haywire when all eyes turn to me, but I plaster a smile on my face and forge forward. *You can do this Lila, just put one foot in front of the other.*

My smile becomes genuine when I see my brother standing at the altar, beaming back at me under the lush, tropical arch filled with fronds and roses. He looks so incredibly happy. He's wearing the same look of joy he did when he told me he wanted to marry Ash after only a few months of dating. I was shocked since it seemed extremely fast to me, but then again, it wasn't like he and Ash were strangers. And I knew from that weekend in Montauk that this was it for them. He told me that he loved her all along, he just didn't understand it before then. And now that he'd experienced loving her in this way, he couldn't imagine his life with anybody else. I thought about those words a lot, and it was obvious to me that Ash and Jake were the real deal. It all fell into place so perfectly after that. Everyone was shocked at how fast they pulled this wedding together, especially our parents. But for me, it only solidified my belief that it was meant to be.

My gaze slides to Jake's right and stops on Alex. He gives me a wink of encouragement. He looks so handsome in the linen suit that Ash picked out for the groomsmen. His hair is gelled perfectly, and I can almost hear his voice in my mind, urging me to keep going. Somehow I manage to keep my eyes fixed on him until I reach my spot, and only then do they land on Lucas. My breath hitches in my throat when I see his face. God, he's beautiful. It literally pains me to look directly at him. He's like a fucking eclipse. Our eyes lock, and I see his Adam's apple bob up and down as he swallows. My heart beats furiously in my chest as I witness a flash of emotion wash across his face. I look away, unable to handle my own emotions simmering under the surface. I try my best to smooth out my features and turn my attention down the aisle. Today is all about the bride.

And right on cue, Ash begins her walk. All the guests stand up to see the bride, but I study my brother's face. He looks awe-struck, as he should be— she looks like an angel floating toward him. Tears prick my eyes; I always cry watching weddings in movies, but here, witnessing the love of two of my favorite people in the whole world, is a totally different ball game. The joy and adoration on both of their faces is something I can only hope someone will wear when looking at me one day.

My eyes hijack my body and track back to Lucas, who's watching me watch them, mirroring what I can only assume is the same expression on my face. I can't believe this is off the table for us now, after dreaming of this exact scene for our wedding my whole life. The beach setting, the twinkle lights, the intimate guest list of only close friends and family. The look of pure devotion in the groom's eyes.

A rogue tear escapes my eye, which I quickly wipe away, hoping it didn't ruin my makeup that took so long to apply. His eyes, still locked with mine, are also glistening. I take a deep breath, unable to pull my gaze away from his. He blinks a few times and slowly drags his eyes away, trying to collect himself. Realizing we're on display up here, I also try to wrangle my emotions and turn my attention back to the happy couple. Thankfully everyone is watching the bride and groom recite their vows, and not paying any attention to us.

When the rings are exchanged, and the officiant announces them man and wife, Jake dips Ashley in a dramatic kiss and all the guests burst into applause. As they saunter down the aisle, Alex offers me his arm and I take it, carefully avoiding Lucas's searing gaze.

As we follow the happy couple, Alex squeezes my hand. "How are you holding up?" he whispers.

I wish I could tell him right here what I saw last night and ask his advice on what to do. But knowing it's not the time or place, I pat his hand and give him my best smile instead. "I'm great," I say. "Now I just have to get through my speech so I can start drinking heavily."

The next hour or so goes by in a flash. We take pictures and take turns sneaking to the bar between setups, to the wedding coordinator's dismay. Fortunately, the photographer must have read the awkward vibe between Lucas and me and does not place us near each other.

After cocktail hour, the bride and groom are introduced and dance to their seats. When the salad is served, it's my cue to get up there and give my toast. I take a deep breath to steady my jangling nerves, wipe my sweaty palms on a napkin and walk over to grab the microphone from the DJ.

Here goes nothing.

I clear my throat into the mic. "Hi, everyone. I'm Lila, the maid of honor and sister of the groom. You all know me; I probably didn't even have to introduce myself." I wince at my shaky start and look around at all the smiling, encouraging faces, carefully avoiding the one face that I know will derail me. Ignoring the somersaults in my stomach, I forge ahead.

"I was stressing about writing this toast for weeks, almost as long as the engagement—and no, this is not a shotgun wedding. Ashley is not pregnant, for all of you wondering."

I get a few chuckles from this, and I turn to face Ash and Jake who are rolling their eyes.

"Anyway, I was stressing so much because, how could I possibly put into words how much I love both of you? But as luck would have it, one night recently I was flipping through the channels on TV and the movie *In Her Shoes* was on. And it was right at the part of the wedding scene where Cameron Diaz is giving the maid-of-honor toast to her sister. She was also having trouble with her own words, so she recited this poem by E.E. Cummings, which is a move I'm going to steal because it could not be more perfect to describe my feelings for you both. So here it goes:

'I carry your heart with me. I carry it in my heart. I am never without it. Anywhere I go, you go, my dear; and whatever is done by only me is your doing, my darling. I fear no fate, for you are my fate, my sweet. I want no world, for beautiful you are my world, my true. And it's you are whatever a moon has always meant, and whatever a sun will always sing, is you.
'Here is the deepest secret nobody knows. Here is the root of the root and the bud of the bud and the sky of the sky of a tree called life; which grows higher than soul can hope or mind can hide. And this is the wonder that's keeping the stars apart. I carry your heart. I carry it in my heart.'"

I pause for a beat and take in the silent, teary audience, then continue on. "I'm also going to steal a line from a birthday card Ash gave me on my eighteenth birthday. 'Love is stumbling through life with your best friend.' Which also could not be more perfect for us, because Ash and I have been doing that for the better part of our existence. So now, dear brother, I give her to you. On the one condition you loan her back to me on a regular basis. So, I guess I shouldn't really use the word 'give,' but more like 'share?'"

More laughs at this.

Jake nods his agreement, and Ash mouths "always" to me, tears streaming down her face.

I bring it home. "So, if everyone could please raise a glass to the beautiful newly wedded couple. I wish you a lifetime filled with happiness, and can't wait to be by your sides through all of it. Cheers."

I lift my glass and take a self-congratulatory gulp, relieved that I pulled it off without passing out in the middle. That actually went fairly well, I hope I didn't make too much of a fool out of myself. The audience seemed to enjoy it, and most importantly the bride and groom.

Ash is up out of her seat and enveloping me in her arms before I can even get down a second sip of my champagne. "That was beautiful, Li." She squeezes me in a bear hug.

Jake walks over and puts his arms around both of us and places a kiss on my temple. "Well done, sis," he whispers in my ear.

I choke back the emotion in my throat and we stand there clinging to each other for a few beats while the DJ starts up again. Alex gets up and starts dancing around us for the comedic relief we all need.

We spend the better part of the next hour dancing like maniacs while most of the guests eat their entrees. I try my best to ignore Lucas and Chloe sitting at their table, but my eyes keep straying to them from the dance floor. They join in for a few songs, and Lucas is gracious enough to keep his distance.

They look like they're having fun together—if not genuinely happy, then at least pretty close to it. Who am I to mess up Lucas's happiness? If she's truly lying about the baby, then he'll find out the kind of person she is eventually. I don't think it's my place to mess this up for him. While they dance, he keeps twirling her and making her laugh, reminding me of what Jamie was doing to me in the bar in Montauk. I feel the familiar pang of guilt as I remember the events of that weekend, and the what-ifs create a tornado in my mind.

A slow song comes on, and Jake grabs my hand before I can protest. How can I resist a dance with my brother at his own wedding?

Alex follows suit, taking Ashley's hand, and starts spinning her around us in circles, grins wide on their faces.

I watch him twirl her around for a beat, then look up to see Jake studying me.

"How are you holding up?" he asks, his eyes flickering with concern.

"I'm fine," I lie, struggling to keep a believable smile plastered on my face.

He scoffs. "Please, Lila. You're my sister, I know when you're not fine," he says with a pointed look.

"Well, it's your wedding! I'm trying to be as fine as I can be." I shoot him a look back.

He sighs. "I appreciate that, I do. You really have been a trooper the last two days. And I'm really sorry I didn't warn you. He didn't give me much time to do so, honestly. But regardless, you've handled it gracefully. And I thank you for that."

I offer him a guarded smile, pleased he can acknowledge how difficult this has been for me. But no matter what, this is his and Ashley's wedding, and of course I can put my drama aside to celebrate them.

I look up and hold his gaze. "Look Jake, you and Ash are the two most important people in my life. This is your wedding. I would do anything for you both. The last thing I want to do is ruin this occasion with my own personal theatrics. And I've tried my best not to put you guys in the middle of it. I know it's been stressful with the wedding and all. My love life drama doesn't even come close to being a priority. I just want to move past it, really," I say to him with certainty and a curt nod of my head. I hope he believes my words, and I don't want to discuss this anymore at his wedding.

He regards me for a beat, then barks out a laugh, shaking his head. "You always put everyone before you. I love that about you—we all do. And one day it'll be your turn, and someone will put you first for a change," he says, grinning at me.

I feel a swell of warmth in my chest at this heartfelt sentiment from my brother, but I can't help but snort at the last part.

He stops moving and looks me in the eye. "You deserve to be happy, Lila. You deserve all of this," he says as he gestures around the room.

I can't help but get a little teary from this rare emotional display from him. I nod, feeling too choked up to speak, and smile at him.

He wraps an arm around me in a hug just as the song ends. "You deserve the world, little sis," he says with one last squeeze, and leaves me to go back to dancing with his bride.

Needing a breather, I slip away to the ladies' room to recoup and check my makeup.

Lucas must have seen me go, because when I walk out of the bathroom he's leaning against the wall, waiting for me.

I stop in my tracks when I see him.

"Hi," he says, eyeing me nervously. The scene on the beach last night replays in my mind. "Can we talk for a sec?" he asks, his tone hopeful.

Yup, déjà vu.

My stomach twists and I do a sweep of the room to see if we have any witnesses. "I really don't know what more there is to say, Lucas. And clearly we cannot be alone together." My tone comes out sharper than I intend it to, and I feel a pang of guilt as he winces at my words.

His cheeks flush, and I know he's thinking about our kiss last night too. He lets out a breath. "I'm sorry about that. I should have never done that. I don't know what came over me," he says, shaking his head.

I feel my own face growing hot and look around, trying to plan my escape. He senses my urge to flee and steps forward to grab my hand. I quickly yank it back like he burnt me. My reaction sends a flash of pain across his face and the pang of guilt in my chest intensifies. My intention isn't to hurt him, but I have no idea how to navigate this situation, and I don't trust myself around him. As much as I want to blurt out my thoughts about Chloe, the look on his face is more than I can bear, and I just can't make it worse.

I sigh, giving in to the anguish clouding his expression. "Okay, just say whatever it is you want to say." I gesture for him to speak.

He inhales and scrubs a hand down his jaw in true Lucas style. "I just wanted to clear the air. I couldn't have you running away from me on the beach last night be how we leave things between us."

I nod, not knowing how else to respond. If it was up to me we wouldn't be leaving anything between us. We'd be on the dance floor, entwined in each other's arms. But instead, he's engaged and (possibly?) having a child with another woman. I flinch at the reality of the situation.

He must read my thoughts flashing across my face. "What are you thinking?" he asks as his eyes study me critically.

Do I tell him what I saw last night? Now is my chance.

"Are you happy?" I ask softly.

His eyebrows jerk in surprise. He was not expecting this question. He looks down at his feet, shifting his weight as he considers how to respond. The confusion on his face clears as he finally settles on an answer. "What's done is done. I made a decision and I'll honor it," he says with conviction, but the sadness in his eyes breaks my heart.

I look at him sideways. "That sounds a lot like 'it is what it is' to me," I say with a smirk.

He lets out a snort. "Yeah, I guess it does," he says as a faint smile brightens his expression somewhat, but doesn't quite reach his eyes.

We stand there and study each other as the moment stretches. My chest feels heavy with defeat as I realize I cannot bear to add to this man's burden. I can't tell him what I saw. I don't want to be the one to ruin what should be the happiest time of his life.

Fortunately, I'm saved from the moment when Ash comes running into the lobby. "Li! There you are. We're about to cut the cake—come back in here!" She frantically motions for us to come back.

I offer him a small smile. "Duty calls," I say, lifting my shoulder into a shrug.

He hesitantly reaches for my hand, and this time I let him. His eyes bore into mine as he speaks. "I'm sorry, Lila. You'll never know how much," he says, his voice shaking.

I give him another nod. "Me too, Lucas."

CHAPTER 19

After getting maybe two hours of sleep, I wake up at five the next morning to go to the airport. Still feeling drunk from the tequila shots Jake made everyone do at the afterparty, I take the quickest shower in history and throw on leggings and a t-shirt. My family and most of the guests are staying for brunch today, but I made an excuse about having to be back for work and not being able to wait till the later flight. I felt guilty about fibbing, but I've reached my limit for emotional turmoil and thankfully nobody called me on it. And honestly, the state I left everyone in last night makes me think not many of them will be making it to brunch, either.

It's too early to say goodbye to anyone, so I slip out of the hotel in the early morning light. My brain is a whirlwind the whole flight home, wondering if I made the right decision. Should I have told Lucas what I saw? My thoughts seesaw between the image of him twirling Chloe on the dance floor, and the look of complete devastation on his face in the hallway. Maybe I should have told him the truth, but he didn't exactly say "no" when I asked if he was happy. He's a good man at heart, and I know he wants to do the right thing. While I have my reservations about Chloe, I really don't know the truth about her condition. So how do I really know what the right thing is? While I wish this wasn't happening, none of it is my business, and the last thing I want is to stick my nose where it doesn't belong.

It's late afternoon by the time I pull up to my house, and I'm so mentally and physically exhausted I could cry. All I want is to crawl into bed and sleep for a week. Which is what I do immediately after I shower the plane off and change into my favorite PJs. I say a prayer of gratitude that I have the house all to myself since my parents decided to extend their vacation for a few days before returning home. I feel such relief I could cry at the prospect of not having to see anyone from the wedding for the rest of the week. I fall into bed and almost immediately fall asleep once my head hits the pillow.

I wake up with a jolt to the shrill sound of the doorbell ringing. I sit up in a panic and look around to orient myself. My room is pitch black and it's dark outside; I have no idea what time it is. I fumble for my phone on the nightstand. 11:52 p.m. Who the hell could be ringing the fucking door at this hour on a Sunday? I sluggishly pull on a hoodie and tie my hair up in a knot on top of my head.

The house is dark; I didn't bother turning on any lights when I walked in hours earlier, so I stumble down the hall till I find a light switch to flick on. I pull open the front door, and there's Lucas leaning against the doorframe.

"What the hell, Lucas?" I say, rubbing sleep from my eyes. I briefly wonder if this is a dream. I hug my arms tight around me, realizing I put my sweatshirt on inside out. Jesus, I must look absolutely insane right now. I self-consciously smooth a hand across the top of my head.

Relief washes across his face. "Oh, thank God you're home," he says.

Where else does he think I would be at midnight after traveling the whole day from Mexico?

"What? What's going on?" I feel my eyes widen. "Is everything okay?" I ask, worried that there is some kind of emergency with my family.

His mouth quirks and he reaches out his hand to calm me. "Yes, yes, everything is okay." He pauses a beat before he speaks. "You know that poem you read during your speech?"

"Huh?" I shake my head, not understanding what the hell is happening right now.

He continues on, mangling the poem from my speech as he attempts to recite it back to me. "'I fear no fate, for you are my fate. I want no world, for you are my world. The root and the bud and the wonder keeping the stars apart.'" He raises his brows. "I carry your heart, Li." He grabs my hand and places it on his chest. "I carry your heart in my heart. Or rather, you carry mine. You will always carry my heart, Lila. Always. I love you." He pulls me in and wraps his arm around me, tucking me under his chin.

I inhale his scent and close my eyes, thinking that yes, this is definitely a dream. I don't move, not wanting to risk waking up.

After a minute, he pulls back and looks at me. "What are you thinking?" he asks, studying my face.

"I'm trying not to wake myself up," I answer plainly.

His face splits into a grin. "Wake yourself up?" He shakes his head, laughing. "This isn't a dream, you goof."

My brow furrows. "It's not?"

"No, it's not." He leans down and touches his forehead to mine.

I close my eyes, not quite sure I believe him. "Are you sure?"

"Lila, look at me," he whispers.

I peek up at him through my lashes.

He reaches out and cups my face with his hands. "This is as real as it gets." He slowly pulls my face toward his, asking permission to kiss me with his eyes.

I open up to him and let him kiss me, still not fully believing I'm awake. I fling my arms around his neck and press myself into him as close as I can get.

He lets out a groan and pulls away from my lips, burying his face in my neck. "Maybe we should go inside," he laughs against my skin.

I take his hand and lead him into the house, flicking more lights on as I go. I stop abruptly as my head clears in the bright kitchen. I turn around to look at him with my hand up. "Wait, I don't understand. What's happening? What about Chloe and the baby?" I ask, my eyes narrowing.

He blows out a sigh and sits on a barstool at the kitchen island, grabbing my waist with both hands. "Turns out she's not even pregnant," he says, slightly shaking his head.

I blink at him, unsure how to respond. Should I act shocked? Pretend I had no idea?

Luckily he lets me off the hook. "I know you know. Ash told me what you saw," he says with a pointed look.

Now I let out a long breath I didn't even know I was holding in.

"After the wedding I needed a minute alone, so I told Chloe I was taking a shower and locked myself in the bathroom. But I just let the water run while I sat on the floor for twenty minutes trying not to have a panic attack. I couldn't stop thinking about you and your speech and how everything you said about Ash and Jake is actually exactly how I feel about you. How I think I've always felt about you, but was just too stupid to realize it. Anyway, I cracked the door open to see if I could sneak out and grab my phone to text you, and I heard her talking to her sister about not having told me yet that it was a false alarm. I just stood there, unable to move, processing her words. After a beat I realized that the only emotion I could actually feel was relief. Such an immense relief that I almost sobbed like a baby." He's smiling so wide at me now that he looks a bit crazy.

"Chloe caught me there staring at her in shock, and I made her admit the truth. Turns out she'd known for a week, but thought if she could come on this trip with me, maybe it would be romantic and she could make me fall in love with her. Or some shit. I don't know, I kind of lost my mind on her after that. We had a big blowout. I told her it was over, that I could never love her. At this point it was like six a.m., and I went straight to your room, but you had already checked out. Jake and Ashley found me on the beach a couple hours later and I told them everything that had happened. That's when Ash told me you saw her drink the champagne," he says, and presses his lips together, eyeing me carefully.

I feel my face get hot. "I didn't know what to do or how to tell you—"

"I know. It's okay, Li—I'm not mad. But now it makes sense why you asked if I was happy. That question really threw me off. I couldn't stop wondering where that came from." He reaches out and pulls me into him. I feel him shaking his head against me. "Of course I wasn't happy. I was doing what I thought was the right thing. The honorable thing. And I would've been fine. But I don't want to be just *fine*. I want to be blissful. I want to be so head over heels in love that I can't see straight." He pulls back and palms my shoulders, eyes locking on mine. "And that's how I feel about you," he says with a grin.

I feel my face split open at his words. These words I've waited to hear from his mouth since I was twelve years old. I lean in and kiss him, and to use his word—it is blissful. His hands tangle in my hair and I crawl onto his lap right on the stool, straddling him. Our kisses get deeper, and a moan escapes from deep inside me. I can't get enough of him.

He reaches up and pulls my hoodie off, and his eyes go wide when he sees what's underneath. I'm wearing a tiny, white sheer tank with no bra. I feel him smile against my skin as he plants little kisses down my chest. He slowly rises from the stool, my legs still around his waist, and carries me up the stairs to my bedroom. *This move is so hot*, I think, and I have déjà vu from our first night together.

He places me down on the bed and reaches behind him to pull his own hoodie off, and the t-shirt underneath goes with it. My hands reach out to touch the hard plane of his bare chest. I still can't believe this is actually happening right now. His eyes blaze with lust, and when they lock on mine fireworks shoot through my insides. He leans down, kissing my cheeks, my nose, my forehead, my

217

mouth, and then he works his way down my torso. He gently tugs off my pajama bottoms and again his eyes bulge when he sees I have no undies on. I giggle at his reaction and he looks up at me, eyes twinkling. I bite my lip and shrug, and he grins at me, shaking his head. "God, you're going to kill me," he softly growls through his throat.

I grab his arms and pull him back up so his face is over mine and try to kick his jeans down with my feet. The corner of his mouth lifts and he helps me, unbuttoning them and sliding them down his legs and off the bed. I feel how hard he is and arch against him, so ready for this. I cling to his body as we rub against each other creating friction, loving how his bare skin feels against my own. The heat of him radiates into my blood and bones.

He groans when he feels how ready for him I am and then stills himself, staring down at my face with apprehension.

"What's wrong?" I ask, scared he suddenly had a change of heart.

He sees the panic in my face. "No, nothing," he says quickly. "It's just... Ah, I don't have a condom on me." He laughs out the last part.

I snort a sigh of relief and shimmy out from under him. I walk to my suitcase in the corner of the room where I tossed it earlier. I fish around for my makeup bag and pull a rogue condom out of the side pocket. I hold it up in triumph and rejoin him on the bed.

He raises a brow. "You brought that to Mexico?"

I shrug a shoulder at him. "You never know who you'll meet on your travels."

He cocks his head as he smirks at me.

I sigh. "Fine, I was hoping for the best possible

outcome. And look! Here it is." I poke him in the chest with a grin.

He laughs as he takes it from me, and reaches down to put it on.

When he resumes his position over me, I latch my legs around his waist crushing him against me. With a groan, he leans his forehead down to touch mine and immediately slips inside me, unable to contain himself.

My breath hitches, and I wrap my arms around his body as he pumps into me. I'm a hurricane of sensation, and it doesn't take long to start feeling the heat build. I am unable to hold back the explosion as it rocks my body.

He follows soon after, calling out my name as his body trembles on top of mine, his face pressed into the side of my neck.

After we both catch our breath, we lay in bed with our legs entwined, Lucas drawing lazy circles on my stomach, me mirroring the motion on his shoulder. My heart is bursting with gratitude at this unexpected plot twist and I can't stop smiling.

"Tell me a secret," I whisper to him.

He turns his head to look at me with such tenderness that I feel my heart clench. I see his eyes light up as his thoughts form in his mind and he clears his throat softly before speaking, his voice coming out raspy. "There was one night, not long after high school graduation, right before I left for college, that I woke up in the middle of the night gasping for breath. I was drenched in sweat, my heart was racing, I don't know if I was dreaming about you or what, but I felt this foreboding doom that I would never see you again. So I went into my closet and started tearing through a bunch of old photo albums, right there in the middle of the night on my bedroom floor. I found one from Christmas a few years before, when your mom got Jake, Alex and me that matching striped polo shirt." He pauses, studying my face to see if I remember.

"We were about fifteen, you must have been thirteen then. Jake, Alex and I had our arms around each other wearing our striped polos and you were right in the middle with the goofiest grin on your face in your Christmas pajamas," he says, eyes shining at me.

I laugh, knowing exactly the photo he's talking about. I remember that Christmas vividly, like it was yesterday.

He smiles at the recognition on my face. "Well, I cut you out of the picture, a little sliver of you that I kept tucked inside the pocket in my laptop sleeve. And after that, every time I felt anxious or scared about the future, I would take out that sliver of a photo and stare at your face —your smile—and I would instantly feel lighter. Because as long as you were somewhere in the world smiling that smile, nothing could ever be that bad. All I had to do was have faith that I'd be reunited with that goofy smile again one day." He leans his head back, lets out a breath and then continues drawing circles on my stomach.

I'm rocked by a wave of emotion and feel tears prick the corners of my eyes.

He must sense it, and he grips his arm tighter around me, squeezing me against him. He tilts his face down again so he can look into my eyes. "It all comes down to you, Lila. It always has, and it always will."

CHAPTER 20

JUNE 2018

I open the door a tiny bit so I can peer through, catching a glimpse of the guys standing at the altar. My heart clenches in my chest as I see Lucas looking so handsome in his tan linen suit, my brother and Alex in matching ones next to him. I smile to myself, remembering the similar scene from Jake and Ashley's wedding almost a year ago now.

Ash catches me sneaking a peek and chastises me, "Lila! Close that door. The first look is supposed to be simultaneous!" She pushes the door shut in my face.

I roll my eyes at her. "I can't help it. He looks so hot in that suit!"

She puts a final coat of gloss on my lips and tucks a rogue wave of hair back in place under my veil. "Are you ready? It's time." She grins wide at me like I can only imagine I looked at her on her wedding day.

"This is so surreal." I shake my head at her.

She laughs, nodding. "If your twelve-year-old self could see you now," she says, and fluffs my dress in the back, making sure the lace falls perfectly.

Her cue to start walking down the aisle begins playing, and she gives my hand one last squeeze before she slips out the door.

My dad takes my hand, beaming at me, and I feel a swell of emotion in my chest. "Let's do it, sweetheart," he says, linking my arm through his. The ushers open the doors and motion for us to start walking.

We move slowly, and I try to take in all the smiling faces of my family and closest friends before my eyes land on the man standing at the end of the aisle. He's looking at me with such love and adoration that my eyes instantly mist up and my breath catches.

My dad stops just before the altar, and Lucas steps down to shake his hand and then takes my own.

"You look beautiful," he says with tears in his own eyes, and we both laugh at each other. We had a bet how long it would take for each of us to start crying. I knew I would be a goner at my first step down the aisle, but we both thought that he would last at least until the vows.

I follow him up to the altar where Alex stands under a beautiful arch of white roses and calla lilies. I look out at the magnificent backdrop of the Atlantic Ocean, its waves crashing below us as the sun makes its descent toward the horizon. My dream of getting married in Montauk is finally coming true. We rented a house right on a cliff overlooking the ocean and set up the ceremony on the back lawn, with a tent on the side for the party after. Just like the wedding we saw that day paddleboarding.

Alex has gotten ordained just for the occasion, and Ash and Jake flank his sides, both smiling at me from ear to ear. As Alex starts his program, I look into Lucas's eyes and am overcome by feelings of joy and gratitude.

He was absolutely right, it all does come down to him.

Love this book?

Don't forget to leave a review!

Every review matters, and it matters a *lot!*
Head over to Amazon or wherever you purchased
this book
to leave a review for me.
I thank you endlessly.

About the Author

Lauren Lieberman was born and raised in Westchester, NY and now lives on the water in Montauk. She is a lover of beaches, sunsets, photography, and of course, rom-com movies and romance novels. A photo editor for People.com by day, she decided to use her free time at night to give writing a try during the pandemic. Down to You *is her first novel.*

Made in the USA
Monee, IL
11 June 2023